Drop Dead, Gorgeous

An Al Pennyback Mystery

Charles Ray

North Potomac, MD

This book is a work of fiction. Names, descriptions, places, and incidents are products of the author's imagination, or are used fictionally. Any resemblance to actual events or persons, living or dead, is purely coincidental.

The reproduction or distribution, by any means, including electronic distribution, is expressly prohibited without the written consent of the copyright holder, except for fair use quotes in connection with reviews.

If you like this book, I'd appreciate your review on your blog, Amazon, or any other book site you desire. And, of course, don't forget to tell your friends about it. Word of mouth is one of the best ways of introducing new fiction to readers.

For information about this and other works of this author, contact the author at charlesray.author@yahoo.com.

Printed in the United States of America.

Drop Dead, Gorgeous

1.

On Fridays, after I close up shop, all I usually want to do is hang out on the couch with my feet up, listening to classical music or jazz on National Public Radio. NPR has some of the best programs going, and I don't have to worry about keeping track of a music collection.

When I lived by myself – which I did for nearly a decade after my wife and son were killed in an auto accident – that was my usual end of week routine. That changed a bit when I met Sandra. Sandra Winter is a school teacher at one of Washington, DC's inner city high schools, and after a week of being cooped up in a classroom with some tough kids from tough neighborhoods, she likes to join me on the couch sometimes, and at other times she likes to go out and indulge herself in the adult pleasure of a fine meal washed down with a glass or two of white wine. I don't mind that myself, except that I tend to wash my food down with a cold beer. When we do go out, we usually end up back at my place, cuddling.

So why, I ask myself, on a Friday evening in late-January, did I find myself sitting in a chilly room in Georgetown that had once been a warehouse, now converted into an exhibition room and stage, watching a parade of bulimic women parade back and forth on a narrow catwalk, showing off clothing that no sane woman would wear, along with yards of flesh?

It had all started when I walked through the door, slapping my upper arms against the chill outside, to find Sandra standing in the middle of the living room with a strange smile on her face, and mischief in her bright blue eyes.

"Al, darling," she said. "You're home early for a change. I hope you're up to going out tonight."

Something in the tone of her voice, or maybe it was the glint in her eyes, made me suspicious. Not that Sandra's the sneaky type, you understand – at least, not normally.

"I'd think after last weekend, you'd want to stay home," I said.

I was probing. The previous Saturday had been Inauguration Day, and despite the fact that Sandra's candidate had lost – or in her words, the court had given the election to his opponent – she felt an obligation to go and stand in the cold along Pennsylvania Avenue with the other gawkers and watch the former

Texas governor get sworn in as the 43d President of the United States. She hadn't gone because she liked that this had happened, but told me she'd never missed an inauguration since coming to the DC area as a college student, and besides, she was planning to join a large group who were there to protest the whole thing.

During the Inaugural Parade, however, someone in her group had pelted the president-elect's limo with eggs, which had spoiled it for her. She didn't like the man or his party, but believed that respect should still be shown the office. Quiet, non-violent protest was as far as she was prepared to go.

She looked sideways at me, as if to see if I was being serious. "I'd rather not be reminded of that," she said finally. "Some people just never know where the limits are. But, there's little chance of anything going wrong with what I have in mind."

Now, it was my turn to look at her out of the corner of my eye. "And, just what pray tell do you have in mind?"

"Well, I was thinking we could grab a bite to eat at one of the restaurants in Georgetown -"

"Whoa, babe," I cut her off. "You know I'm not fond of the tony places in Georgetown. Too many tourists and students and lousy parking – and they charge an arm and a leg for food that's just mediocre. Why in hell would you want to eat there?"

She blushed. She's cute when she blushes. Two little circles of red appeared on her cheeks. Sandra could never be a crook – she has a conscience the size of Mount Rushmore, and simply cannot lie convincingly. I can't believe that I once, very briefly, suspected her of being involved in a murder. When I first met her, I was investigating the shooting death of one of her students, and her neighbor tried to convince me that she was having inappropriate relations with the young man and might have had him killed. What a load of crap that was, and I almost fell for it. But, I digress. She was feeling guilty about something. I gave her a stern look, which only made her blush more.

"Okay," she said. "I do have a specific reason for wanting to eat in Georgetown. Do you remember Calvin Rigg?"

The name didn't register at first. I never forget a face, but names slide off my brain like ducks on a frozen pond. It took a few minutes of concentrated thought for me to remember.

"Oh yeah, the fashion designer who was accused of killing his former partner – hey, you're not talking about what I think you're talking about are you?"

Calvin Rigg's partner Franklin Honeywell had been found in his office with a pair of tailor's shears in his chest. Rigg had been accused of the killing, and had hired me to prove his innocence. Turned out that Honeywell had been killed by his assistant, Albertina Wittmer. I hadn't heard from Rigg since that case, and hadn't missed it. My introduction to the world of fashion hadn't impressed me – a bunch of self-absorbed egos whose view of the world was as warped as plastic sheeting in the hot sun. Not the kind of people I looked forward to spending time with.

Sandra's answer dropped on me like a bag of dog poop. "He's having a showing of his spring line, and he's inviting you and me as VIP guests."

"First you want me to eat in Georgetown. You know I prefer *real* food to the high-tone stuff they serve there. Then, you want me to spend the evening watching a bunch of anorexic women flashing boob and thigh for a bunch of people who 'ooh' and 'aah' but who couldn't possibly wear the rags these women are showing off. That would guarantee to give me a bad case of indigestion."

"Oh, come on, Al," she said, pouting. "You can't tell me you wouldn't enjoy an evening of ogling a bunch of beautiful women."

I stood there, looking at her with my mouth open. The last thing I wanted was an argument. I don't consider myself an ogler – I do like the sight of beauty, but it depends on how you define it. Models have a certain look about them, but it's not what I think of as beauty. Too gaunt, too aloof, too self-absorbed. Of course, I could spend the evening looking at Sandra out of the corner of my eye. Now, she's what I call beautiful.

"Okay, okay, if you insist, but could we stop at the coffee shop in Potomac Village and get a light meal?"

"There's that little Chinese place just off River Road," she said. "That would be preferable to a coffee shop, don't you think?"

Beautiful, smart, and really thoughtful – that's my Sandra.

2.

We stopped at the Chinese restaurant on Travilah Road, just north of River Road, and had chicken with almonds, rice, and Chinese vegetables, washed down with hot green tea.

After supper, we drove to the converted warehouse on South Street in Georgetown. I parked the Green Bug, the Volkswagen Sandra bought me for my fiftieth birthday, in a basement parking garage in an adjacent building.

Sandwiched between M Street, the main corridor running east and west through Georgetown, and the Whitehurst Freeway, an elevated highway running along the Potomac River, South Street and the other narrow streets in the area that formed the south border of Georgetown had once crisscrossed between and among warehouses that were part of the river port. They had long since been converted to office buildings, studios, and exclusive condominiums. There were one or two over-priced restaurants, just as exclusive as the condos, often requiring six months to get a table – *if* you knew the right people. I'd never eaten there. I'm pretty sure my buddy Quincy Chang, a partner in the law firm that has me on a ten thousand dollar a month retainer to do odd jobs for them, knows the right people. Hell, I'm pretty sure he's one of the right people. But, we met when we were both in the army and assigned at Fort Bragg, North Carolina, me in Delta Force and him in the post adjutant general office as an army lawyer, so he pretty much knows my taste in eateries runs mainly to the lowbrow. I prefer paying for food, not ambience.

After coming out of the parking garage, we moved briskly toward our destination. Despite the gentrification of the buildings, street maintenance was no better than in other parts of the city. Mounds of grey slush dotted the sidewalk, and here there were empty wine bottles left behind by the homeless guys who had gone looking for warm grates to huddle over. The cold air did little to erase the smell of sweat, urine and stale booze. Added to that was the biting cold. Thankfully, the inside of the building was heated – the blast of warm air felt great.

The front of the building had been converted into a large entrance lobby, with a ticket booth to the right and an area to the left with tables laden with champagne and an impressive array of finger sandwiches, dips, gourmet crackers, cheese, and fruit. Sandra and I presented ourselves at the ticket booth. The attendant was a tall, skinny redhead with freckles on her nose and cheeks. I gave her my name.

"Oh, Mr. Pennyback," she said. "Mr. Rigg left tickets for you and Ms. Winter." She shoved two tickets to us – front row, 1 and 2. I took them and put them inside my jacket pocket.

"Well, looks like Calvin Rigg still thinks highly of you," Sandra said as she linked her arm through mine. "Front row seats – now that's class."

"I'm more interested in the snacks," I said. "Hell, if I'd known they'd have a spread like this, we could have skipped dinner."

She pulled me toward the table. "Ooh, look – caviar," she said. "I always have room for caviar."

I hadn't noticed the little bowls of the dark eggs sitting nestled among the cheese and crackers. I joined Sandra at the table. She was shoveling crackers piled high with caviar into her mouth and making little sighing sounds. I picked up a cracker and dipped it into the caviar, scooping up a small amount. Not exactly the sophisticated way to do it, but then, I'm not really into sophisticated. She was right, though, it was good.

Despite having eaten, we made a dent in the food near us, and washed it down with a glass each of the bubbly stuff – an expensive French brand. It looked like Rigg was doing well for himself.

A stuffy looking guy wearing a top hat and tail coat, and speaking with a British accent, announced that the show was about to begin before we were able to make complete pigs of ourselves. We followed the rest of the crowd, middle aged men and women decked out in what I'm sure they thought passed for high fashion, but to me just looked like expensive closet hangings, into the large room where the fashion show was being held.

There was a large stage at the back of the room. The runway, a narrow elevated strip projecting from the center of the stage out about fifty feet, had five rows of seats to each side, with each row slightly elevated above the one in front.

Our seats were at the right, just at the end of the runway. Most of the other front row seats were already filled. The house lights went down just as we took our seats. Pink floodlights illuminated the runway, and without preamble or announcement the models began parading from behind the large purple curtains at either side of the stage.

One at a time they pranced and strutted across the stage and down the runway, pausing at the end, and thrusting their hips at the audience on either side, looking at us with stares of aloof disdain.

I'm no fashion expert, but I could tell that Rigg was using African traditional dress for his inspiration, with lots of hip-hugging wrap around skirts and colorful head scarves. I also recognized some of the models from my investigation of his former partner's murder – Bibi Gunn, a tall woman with cocoa brown skin, shiny black hair done in corn rows, and a nice rear end that was displayed to best advantage in the clinging skirts; Svetlana Kalishnakova, the Georgian model with metallic blonde hair, now cut close to her skull, and breasts that threatened to burst from the tightly wrapped blouses, and Genvieve Montand, the Philadelphia native with her brown hair done in a page boy cut. The others were typical fashion models, with long legs, pert breasts, unencumbered by bras, and wooden expressions on their faces.

I had to keep pinching my thighs to stay awake. Two meals, the warmth in the room, and the music – the muted sound of drums to the beat of the models' strutting – made me drowsy. Sandra kept looking askance at me, and occasionally nudged me in the side with her elbow.

The lights came up, and a skinny guy wearing a powder blue tuxedo came out on stage and announced a twenty minute intermission. Sandra and I were halfway to the exit when Calvin Rigg came through the door, heading straight for us. He was wearing faded jeans and a plaid shirt, open at the throat. His hair was still cropped close, and beginning to show gray at the temples. He looked like he'd put on a few pounds since we last met.

"Mr. Pennyback, Al," he said. "I'm so glad you could come. I hope you two are enjoying the show."

"It's amazing," Sandra said.

He looked at me, a faint smile on his pale face. "I imagine it's not your cup of tea, Al," he said. "No matter. I wanted you to come so we could talk."

"What did you want to talk about, Cal?"

"Could we go back to my office? Ms. Winter – Sandra – why don't you enjoy the rest of the show." He smiled at me. "I think you'll be more comfortable in my office."

He had that right. I squeezed Sandra's arm. "I'll be back by the time the show's over, babe."

3.

I followed Rigg toward the left side of the stage, and through a door, into a narrow hallway. We passed the main dressing room. The double doors were flung wide, and inside I could see about a dozen models, in various stages of undress, some getting makeup refreshed – all scurrying to and fro as they prepared for the second half of the show.

He led me to a small door at the end of the hallway. Inside was a modest sized office, with a large mahogany desk at one end, a dressmaker's dummy at the other with pink silk cloth draped over it, several chairs spaced around, and a large cabinet beyond the desk. He went to the cabinet and removed a bottle of Johnny Walker Black and two crystal shot glasses.

"I hope scotch is okay," he said. I nodded,

and he poured two fingers of the amber liquor into each glass. He handed me one, and went behind the desk and sat in a black leather chair.

I took a sip. He sipped, looking at me over the rim of the glass.

"You're probably wondering why I asked you here," he said. "And, why it's taking me so long to get to the point."

I smiled. "I have until the end of the fashion show, so just take your time." I took another sip of Johnny Walker. It went down smooth.

"I had a feeling you weren't a fashionista," he said. He laughed. A deep, throaty chuckle. "Anyway, I have a problem, and I'm hoping you can help me solve it."

"Someone stealing your designs?" I asked.

The question had been asked innocently enough, but this was, I knew, a sore subject for him. His late partner had sued him for stealing *his* designs, which was one of the main reasons he'd been suspected in the man's death. Spots of crimson blossomed on his sallow cheeks.

"No, uh, it's nothing like that," he said. "It's threats."

"You're being threatened? You have any idea who is doing it?"

My money was on a competitor – probably just trying to rattle him and throw him off his game. I'd learned that the fashion industry is as cut throat as the defense industry.

"I'm not being threatened directly. It's more like blackmail," he said. "I received a couple of phone calls – three days ago, and this morning – demanding one million dollars or my business will be destroyed. I have no idea who is behind this. The voice was so distorted I couldn't even tell if the caller was male or female."

Sounded like whoever called him had used one of those voice changer devices. The damn things can be ordered on-line for as little as a couple hundred dollars and they're easy to use.

"What did they threaten to do?"

"What didn't they threaten to do?" He shrugged. "Bollix up my supply shipments, sabotage my computer system – the works. The thing that bothers me, though, is they threaten to harm my models if I don't pay."

That got my antenna up. I might not think of fashion models as potential life companions – or even dates – but, I have this thing about people threatening other people. It pisses me off.

"You think the threats against the models are serious?"

He looked like he wanted to cry. "Some of them have already been contacted and told to stop working for me – or else."

"I'd like to talk to the ones who've been contacted." Just like that, I'd taken the case. No discussion of fee, or even what *he* wanted me to do.

I like puzzles, and seldom turn down a case that has a complicated puzzle to solve. I hate injustice, bullying, or anything that smacks of someone exploiting another person from a position of power. My friend Lucy Mendez, a reporter for the *Washington Post* who has been dogging my trail and writing about me for several years in the Sunday features she does, calls me the Brown Knight. She says I was born a few hundred years too late. Whatever – someone has to be for the little guy who can't help himself.

Rigg knew he had me. "Great," he said. "I'll pay you whatever your usual fee is, for as long as it takes. Just don't let this son of a bitch hurt any of my models." He took a long sip of the whiskey. "I'll go to the dressing room and send the ones who've been contacted here to talk to you."

"One at a time, please," I said.

He nodded, put his glass down, and left. A few minutes later, there was a light tap on the door. I walked over and opened it. Bibi Gunn, dressed in a sheer green wrap around dress that looked like it had been painted on, stood there.

"Hey, handsome," she said in that throaty voice of hers. "Long time, no see."

"Hi, Bibi – you're looking good."

As she squeezed past me and walked toward the chair I'd just vacated, I couldn't keep my eyes off her undulating hips. She glanced back at me over her shoulder, a seductive smile on her face, to make sure I was looking.

"You still look good too," she said. "You still hanging out with that blonde? I saw her with you in the audience."

I acknowledged that I was, and she said 'too bad.'

"I need to ask you a few questions about some threats you've recently received."

The smile vanished. She told me that she'd received a call on January 23d from someone who sounded like he or she had been inhaling helium, telling her to stop working for Calvin Rigg or she would be hurt – and hurt bad. "It scared me," she said. "I mean, really scared me. But, I got bills to pay, and I like working for Cal. You gonna find out who this bastard is, right?"

"I'll do my best. Have you noticed anyone lurking around lately; anything suspicious?"

"Nope, no new faces. Of course, I don't know

who might be in the audience. With the lights in our eyes, we can only see the people on the first rows, and we can't even see them all that well."

She couldn't tell me much more, so I let her get back to the dressing room. Genvieve Montand, smacking a wad of gum now, was next to show up. Despite the French name, she's a Philadelphia girl, accent, attitude, and all.

"Hey, babe, what's up?" she said as she breezed in and perched on the edge of Rigg's desk, flashing me a look at her legs, from bottom to top. "Cal hire you to find out who's threatening us?"

She brushed idly at her close-cropped brown hair, smiling at me with dark brown eyes, but behind the smile I saw something else – fear.

"Yeah – what can you tell me about it?"

"Not much," she said. "Like Bibi, I got a call on the house phone at Cal's studio, like on Wednesday. Strange sounding voice telling me to stop working for Cal, or else. I didn't ask what 'or else' was, if you know what I mean. You gonna find this nut? I mean, it's creeping me out, but I like working for Cal. He treats models nice. A lot nicer than most of the other designers around here."

There wasn't much more she could tell me. We spent a few minutes just chatting, and then she went back to the dressing room to get ready to open the second half of the show.

One of the women I didn't recognize came in next. Victoria del Toro was about five-six, all gentle curves, a complexion like the nougat in the center of a chocolate bar, dark brown eyes that bored into you, full lips that you knew tasted good, and long brown hair that framed an elfin face.

"Ms. Del Toro," I said. "Have a seat." I motioned to the chair in front of the desk. I perched on the edge of the desk.

"You can call me Vickie," she said. She crossed shapely legs, flashing her brown thighs. Models don't seem at all phased by exposed flesh. I'm no model. I locked gazes with her so she wouldn't think I was ogling her legs. I have good peripheral vision, though, so I still got a good look.

"Okay, Vickie. What can you tell me about these threats?"

Her story was the same as the other two, except she'd been called on her cell phone instead of the office phone. She showed me the phone, and called up the list of received calls, scrolling until she got to the date and time of the call, and she showed me the entry; (240) 555-2967, 1/25/2001, 10:30 am.

"That's the number the call came from," she

said.

I took a piece of paper and a pen from Rigg's desk and jotted the number down. Heather, my partner and office manager, could try and trace it on Monday. With luck we'd be able to track it back to a location, or if it was a mobile phone, the owner. It wasn't much to go on, but it beat nothing.

When she left, Rigg came back.

"Did you learn anything?" he asked.

I told him about the phone number, and my plans to try and track it down. He apologized for not being able to send all the models back, but explained that the second half of the show had started, and with the number of costume changes and makeup adjustments, there just wouldn't be enough time. Then, I asked him for a list of the names and contact information for all his models.

"I'll talk to them later," I said.

"Can it wait until Monday?" he asked. "They're all completely wiped out after a show. All they want to do is get out of here and party a while, and then get some sleep. Most of them will be gone within minutes of the last runway walk, and within an hour will be too stoned or drunk to make any sense."

It wasn't ideal, but trying to get information from a bunch of tired and drunk models would be a waste of my time and theirs. I only hoped that whoever was making the threats would take the weekend off.

Charles Ray

4.

The rest of my weekend was a cake walk compared to the trip to the fashion show. Sandra and I rose early on Saturday to clear skies with a bit of nip in the air, but not so cold we couldn't enjoy a four mile run through the woods behind my farm house on River Road in Montgomery County, Maryland, just outside Washington, DC. After the run, we did half an hour on the heavy bag in the barn behind the house, kicking and punching until our arms and legs were tired. I meditated for thirty minutes while Sandra showered, and then after my own shower, we dressed in heavy sweaters and jeans and fixed a huge brunch. Scrambled eggs, fried strips of rib eye steak, diced potatoes with onion and peppers, biscuits, grapefruit juice, and Colombian coffee, which we ate in the living room. We spent the rest of the day snuggled on the sofa listening to music on the radio, getting up only to fix supper around six in the evening, and then turning in at ten.

Sunday was a repeat of Saturday, except for the huevos rancheros, smoked sausage, hash browns, Texas toast, cranberry juice, and Jamaican coffee, which we ate at the little wooden table in the kitchen.

On Monday, the sky was overcast, with the radio forecasting snow, so we did an abbreviated exercise routine – we skipped the heavy bag – and a light breakfast of fried eggs, toast, ham and coffee, before Sandra took off to Carter High School – the inner city school where she teaches – and I hopped in the Bug and drove to the office.

A.E. Pennyback – the 'A.E.' stands for Albert Einstein, thanks to my mother, a fan of the German scientist - Confidential Enquires, the PI firm I operate with the help of Heather Bunche, is located on Fourth Street in Southwest DC, just south of the Waterfront Metro Station. It's on the second floor of an old building that looks a lot like those roadside motels you see in parts of the south – precariously leaning structures with a porch around the ground floor, and a porch wrapping around the second floor. It wouldn't look so forlorn if it wasn't for the towering, shiny condos that hover over it. Part of the gentrification of the Southwest, the glass, steel, and concrete behemoths also block most of my view of the Washington Channel and the Potomac River.

By the time I'd pulled into one of the three spaces that building management has reserved for my business, the temperature had plummeted, and the relative humidity had soared. The cold air bit through my wool parka like a freshly-sharpened hot knife through butter, and the wind scoured my nose, lips and cheeks. I was trying to rub some feeling back into my cheeks when I walked into the reception area that doubles as Heather's office. She had the thermostat turned all the way up, and the blast of warm air felt good.

Heather, her blonde hair cropped close to her skull, sat at her desk, sipping one of her many fragrant teas from a large mug that she held in her left hand, while she pecked away at her computer keyboard with her right. She looked up, smiling. "Hey, close the door," she said. "You're letting all the warm air out."

I slammed the door and leaned against it, letting the warm air massage some feeling back into my hands and face.

"Did you make coffee?" I'm not a tea drinker, and she's finally given up trying to convert me, so she usually brews a fresh pot of Colombian or Jamaican from the supply of fresh ground beans I replenish periodically.

She pointed to the coffee maker on the credenza that sat along the far wall. "It just finished brewing," she said. "You know, you should really consider switching to tea. Less caffeine - and the antioxidants are good for your body.

I know all that, but I *need* that second cup of coffee in the morning. Ignoring her, I filled my favorite mug with the hot, brown liquid, blew on it and took a long swallow. She made a face at me.

"How was the fashion show, Friday night?" she asked.

Now, it was my turn to make a face at her. "Thanks for giving me a heads up on that. You know how I hate events like that."

"I know." She smiled innocently. "Luckily, you were at lunch when Calvin Rigg called, so I gave him Sandra's number. I figured she'd like it. Besides, even though he wouldn't tell me the real reason for his call, I guessed he wanted you to do some snooping for him, but didn't want to talk to you in his office. Was I right?"

My silence was all the answer she needed. She smiled triumphantly. In addition to being a whiz with a computer, Heather reads people almost as well as I do.

"Yeah," I said. "You nailed it. He's being

threatened, and he wants me to find out who's doing it."

"Oh my goodness, *déjà vu* all over again. First his late partner, now him. What is it about the fashion industry?"

"It's not exactly the same," I said. I filled her in on what Rigg had told me, and what I'd learned from talking to the three models. "I need you to run a phone number for me." I gave her the number from Victoria del Toro's cell phone, and the list of Rigg's models. "And, while you're at it, dig into these women. See if there's anything in any of their backgrounds that might cause someone to have it in for them."

"You think one of them might be the actual target – not Rigg?"

"I'm not ruling anything out. It could be one of Rigg's competitors trying to mess up his business. After all, over the past year, he's apparently become quite a force on the Washington fashion scene. Then again, the threat to him could be a red herring, designed to throw everyone off the scent. Right now, I don't know enough. I was thinking I'd make a run to his studio and talk to the other models."

"Don't forget the staff," she said. "Remember Tina Wittmer."

I could never forget her. Franklin Honeywell's assistant, she was a designer wannabe, and a coke addict. When he started using her designs without giving her credit, she killed him. When I first met her, she seemed like a quiet, not unattractive, but somewhat mousy girl who wouldn't hurt a fly. I'd almost been caught sleeping on that one.

"Good idea. I'll get the names when I talk to Rigg. I'll need you to run a full background on them as well. Oh, and while you're at it, see if you can find out who his main competitors are – check them out as well."

She was beginning to run Internet searches as we spoke, her tea all but forgotten. There wasn't much for me to do, so I shucked my jacket and went into my office.

My office is a bit smaller than the reception area – a real bare bones space, with an old surplus executive desk I bought at an army auction, a leather executive chair behind the desk for me, and a wooden chair in front of the desk for visitors – that I usually preferred to let stay out with Heather, a credenza behind my chair, and two three-shelf book cases containing phone books, crime reference books, and a few travel magazines. The walls were relatively bare – a couple of hunting prints that Heather had bought for me, and an autographed photograph of me with former Chairman of the Joint Chiefs of Staff Colin Powell, taken when I was a lieutenant colonel assigned to the Pentagon – a few years before I retired from the army.

I plopped down in my chair, my back to the window. Not much to see in the winter. The bare trunks of the trees planted among the condos that sat there like hulking silver beasts, blocking my view of the channel and river. During the warm months I at least had the lush green of the trees to look at.

Nothing much to do, so I switched on my computer. When the screen quit flashing and settled down, I signed in to check my emails. Mostly spam, so I just checked and deleted everything. I then opened up the online chess program that I frequently play – I never win, but the perpetual optimist, I'm always trying.

I'd managed to get my King out of check after twenty moves, with no real place to go and the possibility of being mated in four more moves, when Heather poked her head through the door.

"Hey, boss," she said. "I got information on that phone number you gave me, but you're not going to like it – it was a disposable phone."

Damn! Disposable, or burner, phones, cell phones that are bought, used, and then junked, are the favorites of drug pushers and other miscreants who don't want to be traced. "Any chance of tracking where it was sold, and to whom?"

"It was part of a shipment to a Best Buy in Frederick, Maryland," she said. "I called, and their records indicate that it was sold a month ago, but the buyer paid cash, and no one remembers who bought it."

"And, since it's not part of a phone account, it'll be hard to find out if it was used to call anyone else unless they have a cell and capture the number. Well, I guess I'll just have to deal with this case the old fashioned way."

"You mean, twisting arms and cracking heads?"

"I hope it doesn't come to that." I laughed. She and I both knew I didn't go in for coercive methods of getting information. When she can't dig it up, I much prefer tricking people into telling me what I want to know. "No, I mean hitting the bricks and asking lots and lots of questions."

"You want me to help?"

Ever since she'd gotten her PI license, she'd been anxious to get out into the field. But, she was far more valuable at her desk, coaxing information out of her computer or over the phone from one of her many contacts among the secretaries and personal assistants of the people who count in the DC area.

"No, not now," I said. "You keep digging into those backgrounds. I'm paying a visit to

Georgetown."

"So, you're going to spend more time with those beautiful models?"

"Oh, yeah." I grimaced. "It'll be like going to the dentist for a root canal. Have you ever tried talking to one of these women?"

"Come on, Al," she said. "You're sounding like a dyed in the wool chauvinist. Not all of these women are empty headed fools."

"Okay, you're right. Some of them are quite smart. But, getting them to focus on something besides fashion is . . . well, let's just say they're not the most fascinating people to talk to."

"I think being threatened might help focus their minds on something besides fashion, don't you?" She cocked her head and gave me one of her patented glares.

Of course, she was probably right. She usually is.

5.

I asked Heather to type up a contract for Rigg to sign – our usual rate of five hundred bucks per day plus expenses. While she was cranking that out, I called Rigg to have him clear his calendar for the morning. I planned to talk to everyone even remotely connected with his studio. While I was at it, I asked for the names of the non-models working with him, a total of six people. I wrote the names down, told him I'd see him within the hour, and grabbing my jacket, went to Heather's desk.

We exchanged papers, she handed me the contract, all neatly typed, and in two copies, while I handed her the list of names, six hastily scribbled names on the back of a receipt for gas that I'd found in my top desk drawer.

"Why don't you tell me when you run out of notebooks," she said, as she smoothed the receipt out and recopied the names into a steno pad she keeps near her keyboard.

"I need a notebook," I said.

She made a growling sound and glared at me. I pulled on my jacket and got the hell out of her sight.

The weather had turned as cold as Heather's expression. The wind blowing off the river had picked up, tossing pieces of paper along the street and causing people to huddle in their coats as they lowered their heads into the gusts.

I let the bug's engine run until the heater had taken most of the chill out of the air, and the steering wheel no longer felt like a block of ice. It was after nine-thirty, and I'd estimated twenty minutes from my office to Georgetown. The trip took nearly an hour. The temperature drop had frozen the slush on the streets and sidewalks, creating traffic gridlock throughout the District. We get snow and ice every year, but drivers in the DC area never seem to learn how to navigate during such conditions. At the first sign of ice on the roads, they freak out. From my office to Rigg's studio was about nine miles, Maine Avenue to Independence Avenue, around the Lincoln Memorial to Twenty-Third Street, then north to Pennsylvania Avenue – a few more blocks to M Street, then west into Georgetown. Nine miles during a time of day when traffic should normally be relatively light and I saw five accidents – most caused by some idiot forgetting that if you stamp on the brakes when you're driving on ice, your car will skid – it's unfortunate they don't give tickets for driving while stupid.

The traffic had been terrible before I hit the strip of bars and boutiques on M Street in Georgetown, but it was a snap compared to the near gridlock of students, many driving their first cars, and tourists on that stretch of throughway. You might not think tourists visit the national capital in winter, but, you'd be wrong. The number of out-of-state plates on cars on that few block stretch of street was unbelievable, with drivers pulling out of parking spaces without looking, or suddenly stopping to gawk at the signs – it took me nearly twenty minutes to navigate the six blocks from the bridge across Rock Creek to Wisconsin Avenue, and then another five minutes waiting for clearance to make the left turn down toward the river.

Thankfully, after the turn, the traffic was lighter. Of course, the streets were also worse, with almost more potholes than pavement. I made the right turn on South Street, and found space in the parking garage next to the building in which Calvin Rigg had his studio.

The entrance foyer of his building hadn't changed much since my last visit. The same bored-looking receptionist who doubled as a guard, and who didn't seem to care anymore than before who entered – she waved me to the elevator without even looking at my ID.

I was caught by surprise, therefore, when the elevator doors slid open on the second floor. Gone were the double glass doors. The elevator opened onto a large open space. A glass-top desk sat in the center, and behind it was a large sign, *Rigg's Rigs*, in tasteful gold letters etched into a large glass rectangle. The walls had photographs and prints of skinny models wearing fashions that I assumed were Rigg's designs, and mannequins on white plastic stands were dotted around the room. Odd-shaped chairs were spaced around the room. A young blonde with an overbite and large breasts encased in shimmering blue silk sat behind the desk playing with an ultra-modern phone console. She looked up and smiled when I stopped in front of the desk.

"Yes," she said in a soft voice. "May I help you?"

I showed her my ID. "I have an appointment with Calvin Rigg."

"Yes, Mr. Pennyback. Please have a seat. Cal will be with you shortly." She motioned toward one of the odd chairs.

I decided to stand. I walked around, looking at the mannequins and pictures.

"Al, come on back." Rigg came through a door in the rear wall that I hadn't even seen. He motioned me to follow, holding it open. "Lots of changes since you were here last."

"You seem to be doing all right for yourself," I said.

"Yeah, I guess you could say I made a comeback. It wasn't easy, though. Even though you proved my innocence, there were those who for a while treated me as if I was contagious." We were in a wide hallway, stacked high with boxes. He turned right and led me down the hallway to a door on the left. "My designs finally caught on, though, and now I'm doing quite well – so well in fact that I had to expand. We're now on this floor *and* the floor above."

"I'd call that quite a comeback. You're the top fashion designer in the city now, eh?"

He opened the door and stepped aside to let me enter. His office was *big*. A large executive desk opposite the door, with a leather and suede executive chair, a wet bar to the left, with a good selection of liquors in the shelf over it, a bookcase to the right, filled with magazines and books – and some of the books were expensive looking – and a drafting table just inside to the right of the door. He walked past me, smiling at me.

"Actually, my designs are beginning to catch on even in New York. If things work out, I'll have a showing up there in spring."

"What could go wrong? You seem to be on top of the world right now."

His smile faded. He motioned me to a leather chair to the side of the desk, and walked to the bar. "Can I offer you a drink?" I shook my head. He poured two fingers of scotch in a crystal glass and sat behind his desk, frowning into his drink. "I'm doing well. But, if whoever is threatening my models causes them to bail on me, it could bollix things up. I have three more shows coming up, and they'll be watched by the people in New York. If they're a bust . . . well, you know how these things work."

I didn't really. The fashion industry is foreign to me. I imagined, though, that if his shows in DC bombed, for whatever reason, he'd have a hard time getting a toehold in New York City, the fashion capital of North America.

"So, if your models quit, that would sabotage your shows. Can't you just hire new ones?"

He took a sip of scotch, making a wry face as if he didn't like the taste. "If only it was that easy," he said. "When a designer blacklists a model, it's almost impossible for her to get another decent job, you know. But, every coin has two sides. When models start bailing on a designer, it's like he has a contagious disease. It becomes pretty difficult to hire good models. If I don't have the best models, my shows are lame – and, you know what they do with lame horses. Well, they pretty much do the same to lame designers."

"In that case," I said. "I'd better get cracking on finding out who's trying to bring you down. I'd like to start with talking to the rest of the models, and then the staff."

He put the glass down, and pushed it away, frowning. "Funny, you'd think I'd like this stuff. I have to go to so many functions where you're expected to drink, so I drink it. Actually, I hate it." He took a deep breath. "The models and most of the staff are on the floor above. My assistant, the receptionist, and a guy I hired to clean the place are down here with me. I'll take you up."

I put a hand on his arm. "No, maybe it would be more efficient for me to talk to the people on this floor first," I said.

He nodded. "Makes sense – fewer people. Who do you want to talk to first?"

"Let's start with your assistant, but first give me a little background on her."

"Him," he said. "My assistant's a man. I had a woman, the best in the business, but she was run over by a hit-and-run driver three months ago, and I had to hire a replacement. This guy's pretty good, but I still miss Stella. I'll take you down the hall to his office."

I followed him out of his office, and down the hallway, past two doors to a door at the far end. He rapped lightly on the door and pushed it open.

A small man, dressed in chinos and a brown turtleneck sweater, sat behind a small wooden desk, flipping papers in a brown cardboard file folder. He had a pale complexion, narrow nose, and thin lips. His eyes, dark brown, were almond shaped and spaced widely to either side of his nose, under thin brown brows. The dark brown hair covering his bullet-shaped head was combed straight back. As we entered, he looked up, a faint smile on his face.

"Cal," he said in a high pitched voice. "What can I do for you?"

"Jason, I'd like to introduce you to Al Pennyback," Rigg said. "He's a private investigator I've asked to look into these threats the models have been receiving. He'd like to ask you a few questions if you're not too busy."

He gave me a look that was unreadable – part nervous, part curious – scanning me from head to foot. "Sure, Cal . . . although, I don't know much about it other than what I've heard the girls saying." He motioned at a straight backed chair at the side of his desk. "Please have a seat, Mr. Pennyback."

"Give me a call when you're done," Rigg said. "And I'll introduce you to the others."

I waited until Rigg had gone, and then took out my notebook. "Mind if I ask your full name?" I asked.

"Lane, Jason Lane," he said. "Like I said, though, I really don't know too much."

"You never know," I said. "Sometimes, the most insignificant thing to you can be useful. Let's start with some basic background. How long have you worked for Calvin?"

"Just under three months. I moved to Washington four months ago, and was looking for work. Calvin's former assistant was unfortunately killed in an auto accident, and he advertised for a replacement. I applied, and luckily he hired me."

"What are your duties?"

He laughed. "Oh, I do just about everything. I order supplies, keep the books, make appointments. Anything that takes Calvin away from what he does best – designing clothes – is my job."

"Do you get involved in the design at all?"

"Man, what I know about designing clothes you could put in your eye, and it wouldn't even make you blink. I'm just a paper pusher. I have a degree in accounting, and before I came here I worked as a bookkeeper at an auto repair shop."

Quite a leap, I thought, from doing paperwork at an auto body shop to doing it at a human body shop. But then, I guess paperwork is paperwork regardless of the industry.

"I take it you haven't received any threats yourself?"

"No," he said. "As far as I know only the models have."

"What have they told you about it?"

"Not much – just that they get these calls telling them to quit working for Calvin – or else. The calls apparently come in at all hours; some on the office phone, some to their cells."

"Have any of them quit?" I asked.

"Not yet." He frowned. "Calvin's the best designer in town – some say the best on the East Coast. Models are lined up for a shot at wearing his designs. Of course, some of them seem to be getting antsy, so I imagine it's just a matter of time until one or two get so scared they'll take the chance on being unemployed. If that happens, it'll open the floodgates. If models start quitting on a designer, it's the kiss of death."

That's usually how it works. You find the weakest link and push him – or her – over the edge. People are natural followers. One goes, and pretty soon the pressure builds, and others follow.

"Okay," I said. "Thanks for talking to me. I need to talk to the others who work on this floor."

"I'll take you back to Calvin's office -"

"That won't be necessary. I can find my own way. Where can I find the janitor?"

I didn't figure a cleaning man would know much, but I liked to cover all bases. Then, I'd chat with the receptionist, who would be the one who first answered the calls to the office phone.

He looked skeptical, but was obviously accustomed to following orders. "The janitor is usually in the first office down the hall – more of a broom closet actually – when he's not cleaning things."

I thanked him and left. The first door was ajar, so I pushed it open. A fat, middle aged man wearing a blue cotton jumpsuit sat on a stool in the center of the room reading a wrinkled *Washington Post*. He looked up as I entered, his brows arcing upward. "Uh, can I help you?"

"Are you the sanitation engineer who works for Calvin Rigg?" I asked.

He laughed, his belly jiggling under the jumpsuit. "Hell no," he said. "I'm the janitor. I keep the place sanitary, but I ain't no engineer."

I took a liking to him – a man who called things what they were instead of pinning euphemisms to them. I showed him my ID and told him why I was there. "What can you tell me about the threats people have been getting?"

"I don't know nothin', really. I hear people talkin', but they ain't talkin' to me. "Cept for Mr. Rigg, I'm just plain invisible to the folk that work here."

"Yeah, but that's like air," I said. "You can't see it, but try to get along without it. I'll bet this place would fall apart if you left."

He smiled broadly, puffing out his chest.

"Tell me about it. Nowadays, I'm the first one in here, and the last one out."

"Nowadays?"

"Uh huh," he said. "Before the Lane kid came, Mr. Rigg's assistant was a woman named Stella. She used to come in early too – sometimes she'd even beat me in – and she stayed after everybody left. Stella was like everybody's mother, you know. She fixed coffee, listened to problems – sometimes she even fixed 'em. She got run down by a car one mornin' not far from her house. They never found the son of a bitch that run her down.

His eyes misted over and his mouth turned down in a hang dog look.

"Now, there was somebody coulda told you what was goin' on 'round here. Everybody talked to Stella – told her everything. I really miss her."

I'd never met the woman, but I found myself wishing she was still there as well. Of course, wishing never makes it so. It just meant that I'd have to work a little harder to get to the bottom of things.

"Well, anyway," I said. "Thanks for taking the time to talk to me. If you do hear anything, I'd appreciate it if you'd let me know."

"You can count on it." He said it like he meant it.

I left him there thumbing through the wrinkled newspaper, a sad look on his face.

I walked back out to the reception area. The well-endowed blonde was hunched over a fashion magazine. Her lips moved as she read the article. When my shadow fell across the page, she looked up, frowning at first, then a broad smile lit up her face.

"Yes, Mr. Pennyback," she said. "What can I do for you? Calvin said you might want to talk to me."

I sat on the edge of the futuristic plastic

chair near her desk, taking out my notebook.

"Could we start with your name, and how long you've worked here?" I asked.

"Tillie," she said. "Tillie Moyers. I've been Cal's receptionist for just over a year now."

"I guess that means you're pretty familiar with what goes on around here." She nodded, and then shook her head. "You're familiar, or you're not – which is it?"

"Sort of, but I don't pry, you understand." She looked down at her bosom. "I'm not exactly model material. They like the slightly undernourished look. And, the other girls don't talk to me all that much."

I could see that *some* women might a tad jealous of her endowments. Added to that, she didn't strike me as too bright.

"Do all phone calls come through your console here?"

"Calvin has a direct line in his office," she said. "But, all the other calls come through here."

"So, you're aware of the threatening calls to the models."

She looked confused. "Uh, sort of – I mean, after the fact sometimes. I hear them talking about it."

"The times that you *are* aware of them, do you remember anything about them?"

"Only that they asked for the models by name," she said. "So, I figure it must be somebody who knows them."

"What can you tell me about the voice? Do you recognize it? Was it a man or a woman?"

The look of confusion deepened as she smiled up at me. "Not really. The voices were kind of funny, you know – like you get when you breathe helium at a party. Kind of squeaky like a cartoon character. You can't tell if it's a man or a woman."

"Did it occur to you that someone calling and disguising their voice might be up to no good?"

"Shoot, I don't know what kind of people these models hang out with. I get paid to answer the phone and transfer the calls."

I could only sit there and look at her. What a piece of work, I thought. I didn't even bother asking if she'd thought of calling the police or anything – I was afraid trying to answer me might cause her head to explode.

"Okay, look – if you get any future calls like this, take notes, try to get the caller to give you a name or reason for calling, and then get in touch with me." I gave her one of my cards. She looked at it as if it was a snake, but then took it.

"What if the caller won't answer my questions?" she asked. "Do I still put the call through?"

"Yeah, go ahead and put the call through," I said. "But, if you can, stay on and monitor it, and make a note of what the caller says."

She frowned up at me. "But, that would be an invasion of privacy. Won't I get in trouble for doing that?"

"Look, you and I are the only ones who know you'll be doing it," I said. I took a deep breath. "I won't tell anyone you did it – okay?"

"Well, okay. I guess if you're telling me to do it, and Calvin's okay with it."

I reached over and patted her hand, which earned me a smile and a fluttering of her lashes. I decided to stop talking to her before *my* brain exploded.

6.

I asked Tillie for directions to the models' rooms. She began giving me convoluted instructions about going back to the hallway, and finding a fire door that opened to the emergency evacuation stairs, but I cut her off and asked if I could get there by way of the elevator. She nodded. I thanked her and headed for the elevator.

The last sight I had of her as the elevator doors slid closed - she was sitting there staring at the open magazine on her desk, looking confused.

A few seconds after they closed, the doors slid open. I looked out on a large room. To the right were a desk and a row of large three drawer cabinets. A medium brown skinned man with a completely bald head and a pointed goatee sat behind the desk reading the day's *Post*. To the left were two smaller desks – each with a sewing machine in the center, two large wooden tables with scraps of fabric littering the tops, five headless dress mannequins, and rolls of fabrics of all kinds and colors were stacked against the wall. A woman sat behind each desk, working away at a sewing machine. One was a very dark skinned woman with broad shoulders and black hair done in cornrows; the other was a narrow-shouldered woman with unnaturally pale skin and sandy brown hair. Metal folding chairs sat near each of the three desks, and more were folded and leaned against the wall – utilitarian, rather than to impress visitors.

The man looked up as I approached. "You looking for Calvin Rigg," he said. "His office is the floor below. If now, you're in the wrong place. Only employees are allowed on this floor."

I flipped open my wallet, showing him my ID. "I just left your boss," I said. "Now, I'm up here to talk to the people that work on this floor about these threats your models have been getting."

He turned back to his newspaper, but when I didn't move on, he looked back up at me frowning in confusion. "Uh, you want to talk to me?"

I took my notebook out and turned the metal chair around, sitting with my elbows on the back. "I'm talking to everyone who works here. Let's start with your name."

His eyebrows arched up, and the frown deepened. I stared back at him, my pen poised over the open notebook. He was too small to try playing chicken with me – and, his brain eventually processed that fact.

"Greg Cheney," he said. "And, there's no relation to the dude in the White House."

That, I thought, was supposed to be some kind of standing joke. I didn't smile.

"What do you do here, Mr. Cheney?" I asked.

He looked disappointed that I hadn't picked up on his lame attempt at humor.

"I do makeup."

That made him the person who put all the strange faces on the models for shows, which meant he had contact with every one of them. I couldn't imagine they talked too much when their faces were being painted, but then again, maybe they did.

"Do the models talk to you about personal things?" I asked.

"When I'm putting on their makeup, they don't talk much, and I wouldn't be listening anyway. I have to pay attention to what I'm doing, you know. Wouldn't do to get an eyebrow line crooked – it could ruin the whole show." He certainly had a high opinion of his value to the fashion business. "Sometimes, though, they chat just before I start application, or after I'm done.

He cocked his head, looking at me as if waiting for my approval. I held the pen over the page, looking at him coldly.

"Uh, yeah," he said. "Sometimes they tell me personal stuff. 'Course, you want to know about the threats, right? A couple of them – Bibi and Michelle – mentioned getting calls from some creep with a strange voice. Michelle got hers just before I was to put on her makeup. She was so freaked and shaking, I could hardly get her eye shadow on."

It occurred to me that if someone wanted to bring Rigg's operation down, getting rid of the makeup technician, or one of the other support people would accomplish it.

"Have you ever received any threats?" I asked.

"Nope, and frankly I thought Bibi was just pulling my leg. I wouldn't have believed it if Michelle hadn't been so messed up, you know."

"So, you think the threats are serious?"

"Don't matter what I think," he said. "If the girls take it seriously, it's serious." He inclined his head toward the two women across the room. "Now, if you really want the gossip about what goes on in this place," he said in a quiet voice. "You need to talk to those two. Ever since

Stella got killed by a hit-and-run driver, they've been the ones the models talk to. When they're dressing them, they never stop talking."

"Okay, but I might have a few more questions for you later," I said.

I stood and walked over to the two women who had stopped working with their sewing machines and were watching me.

"Didn't get much help from Greg, did you?" the black woman said. "You're just wasting time talking to the men around here."

"That's for sure," the pale one said. "The girls don't tell men what's on their mind."

I sat on a folding chair near the black woman, and put my notebook on the table. "So, I need to talk to you, eh? Okay, let's start with your names and go from there."

"Lisa Farnsworth," the black woman said.

"Martha Franks," the other one said.

I wrote their names at the top of the page. "And, what do you two do here?"

They looked at each other, smiling.

"We keep this place running," Farnsworth said. "We cut and sew up Calvin's designs."

"And, we make sure the dresses fit the models," Frank added.

"Without us, this place would dry up and blow away," Farnsworth said.

There was no break between one stopping and the other starting. It was like listening to one person with two different voices.

"What can you tell me about the threats?" They squared their shoulders and leaned forward. I held up a hand. "And, one at a time, please. Ms. Farnsworth, how about we start with you?"

Frank frowned and sat back, folding her arms across her flat chest.

With a knowing smile, Farnsworth leaned forward, fixing me with a piercing glaze of her dark brown eyes.

"Well, as far as I know, the calls started about a week ago, would've been January 22d. I think Bibi got the first call. She thought it was some kind of prank until Svetlana got called, and then Genvieve. After that, the others started getting calls, so they started taking it seriously."

"Hmph," Frank said. "I'm not so sure these gals are capable of really taking anything seriously."

Farnsworth laughed. "You got a point there, girl. They are all a little light in the brains department."

The two of them were enjoying themselves entirely too much. I held up a hand to stop them. "Hold on, ladies," I said. "You're not trying to tell me you think this is some kind of prank, are you?"

They both frowned at me.

"Of course not," Farnsworth said.

"No way," Frank said. "It's serious enough all right."

"But, what is the caller trying to achieve by threatening models?" I asked.

"Beats me," Farnsworth said. "Calvin seems to think it's being done to drive him out of business."

"Pish," Frank said. "Models are a dime a dozen. There are more women in this town wanting to be models than jobs to hire them. For every one that quits, there's two lined up to replace her."

Farnsworth nodded, looking serious. "If whoever this person is really wanted to hurt the business, he'd get rid of the makeup artist." She shot a frown toward Greg Cheney. "A *good* makeup artist is hard to find."

Frank laughed. "But, not impossible," she said. She made a face at Cheney, who stuck his tongue out at her. "Now, if you really want to hurt a designer, you get rid of his seamstresses."

"Oh, yeah," Farnsworth chimed in. "There aren't that many top rated cutters in this town. And, Martha and I are *the* best. If we were to quit, Calvin would be up a creek without a paddle, that's for sure."

While she was talking, out of the corner of my eye I saw the door in the rear of the room open, and Jason Lane walked in. He was carrying a bunch of long sheets of paper in his hand. The two women, now well into their recitation, ignored him.

"Oh, that is *so* right," Frank said. "*We* are what keep this business going – aside from the designer himself, of course."

Lane walked over and dropped one of the sheets of paper on the table. "This is the list of designs Calvin wants for the next show, ladies," he said. "I'll be picking up the special fabric this morning, so you'll need to get to work right away to make sure they're ready – we only have two weeks."

Farnsworth picked the paper up, gave it a cursory glance, and handed it to Frank. "This doesn't look all that complicated," she said. "You get the fabric and we'll have these dresses sewn up in four or five days." She turned her attention back to me. "Like Martha was saying, it's us seamstresses who really keep things humming in this business. Ain't that right,

Jason?"

Spots of red blossomed on Lane's cheeks. "Uh, I guess so," he said.

"You guess so? Boy, you for sure are no Stella," she said.

"That's true," Frank said. "Now, there was a woman who knew more about this business than even Calvin. *She* would've known what we're talking about."

"It's just my job to keep the paperwork in order," Lane said. His cheeks darkened even more. "I'd like to see how you made out if I didn't get your paychecks processed on time."

"Aw, chill out, hon," Farnsworth said. "We're just having a little fun at your expense. We know you do a good job. It's just that we miss having Stella around to talk to. Everybody loved talking to that woman."

"Yeah," Frank said. "She was kind of our den mother, rest her soul."

"Hell, all you broads did was sit around and gossip," Cheney said from across the room. "Taking about your periods, and how big or small your last man was. Huh!"

Lane's face was now entirely red, and he looked like he wanted to crawl away somewhere.

"Uh, I have to go," he said. "I have some paperwork to finish before I go pick up that fabric."

He scurried back through the door as if someone was chasing him. Cheney and the two women laughed so hard they had tears in their eyes. I felt sorry for the poor kid.

"Look, thanks for talking to me," I said. "I think I'll go back and talk to the rest of the models. I assume they're all here today?"

Three heads bobbed up and down in unison. I followed Lane through the back door. By the time I got there he was nowhere to be seen.

Behind the door was a long, fairly wide hallway with five doors set in the walls on each side, and what looked like a smallish room at the end. I could see a counter with a microwave, and the end of a table. There was a white card on each door. I looked at the one to the right. It had Bibi Gunn's name on it. The one on the left had Victoria del Toro's name. From what I'd just heard outside, I figured the first two dressing rooms were the best of the lot, and reserved for Rigg's star models. I wasn't sure that having two competitors so close to each other was a good idea, but I suppose Rigg knew something I didn't. I'd already talked to the two of them, so I moved on to the next door on the right. The name on the door was Li Ming Tang. I rapped on the door.

"Come in," a muffled voice said.

Li Ming Tang was tall. And, she was built. She had milky skin that looked like fine porcelain, an oval face, dark, wide-set almond eyes, and silky black hair that draped her face and hung down as far as her small, pointed breasts that bobbed beneath the T-shirt she wore. Her legs, sticking out of a pair of black shorts – that were *short* – were the same color as her face and arms, and were long and shapely. She sat slouched on her chair, painting her fingernails a dark, almost black, red color. She looked up as I came in. When she smiled, it was as if someone had turned up the lights in the room – and the heat.

"Li Ming Tang?"

Okay, maybe I might have missed the name card on the door, but I sounded stupid to me. She didn't seem to notice.

"Yes," she said in a throaty voice. "You must be al Pennyback, the detective Calvin hired to find out who is threatening us."

Making an effort not to stare at her crotch, where the shorts clung tightly to her flesh, I sat on the edge of her dressing table.

"That's me," I said. "Have *you* been threatened?"

"Yes, I received a call too. The night before the show – that would have been on Thursday, the 25th."

"Where were you when you were called?"

She frowned – little furrows forming between her eyes. "I was at home," she said. "The call came at ten, just as I was about to go to sleep."

"On your home phone?"

"No, I don't have a, what do you call it, landline," she said. "It was on my cell."

"Did you recognize the caller?" I asked.

"No, it didn't sound like a real person." She shook her head. "Funny sound, you know, like maybe talking with something over mouth."

Reaching past me, her hand brushing my thigh, she picked her purse up from the floor. She withdrew a pink sequined cell phone from the purse and flipped it open. She pushed the buttons, nodded, and held it up so I could see the number, date and time - (240) 555-2967, 1/25/2001, 9:58 pm. The same cell that had called Victoria del Toro. I made a note in my book.

"Do you remember what the caller said?"

"I can't forget it," she said. "If you want to live, you'll quit modelling for Calvin Rigg is what he said, then hung up."

"You think the threat was serious?"

She shook her head, fixing me with her dark almond eyes. "Maybe, maybe not," she said. "No matter. I need this job."

The determined set of her face said she meant it. Whether it was bravery or desperation, or a combination of both, she wasn't about to jump ship. I admired her, and thought at the same time that she was being foolish. If the caller was serious, she could be in danger.

"Okay," I said. "Thanks for talking to me. Let me know if you get any more calls."

"You gonna stop this?"

It was a simple question, but I detected a slight note of fear in her voice. So, it was desperation that caused her to refuse to quit. Well, I'd just have to find whoever was doing this – and fast, before anyone got hurt.

"I'll do my level best," I said.

I left her there, and crossed the hall. Svetlana Kalishnakova's name was on the card. I tapped on the door and pushed it open, catching the Georgian just pulling a sweater over her short blonde hair. Her ample breasts swung free. As the neck of the sweater dipped below her eyes, she looked up at me and winked.

"You like vat you see?" she asked.

I didn't *dislike* it, but I was working. Besides, she was a bit too brassy for me, even if I'd been looking for companionship – which I definitely am not. Sandra is all I need. I just smiled at her.

"You know why I'm here?"

She pouted.

"Unfortunately for me, yes," she said. "You vant to know about threats. Yes, I get threat, too. Strange voice call me Friday morning here at studio. Tell me to stop work for Calvin or I maybe have accident."

"Did you get the call on your cell phone?"

"No. Call came on phone in break room."

I noted it all down. "Are you planning to quit?" I asked.

She ran her long, manicured fingers through her spiky hair. "I don't think so. I have too much bill to pay, and if I quit it be hard to get another job."

There wasn't much else to get from her, so I thanked her, asked her to get in touch if she got another call, and left.

My next stop was across the hall. Name on the tag on the door was Jessica Clooney. I tapped on the door and waited.

"Come in," a small, quiet voice said.

I pushed the door open. Jessica Clooney was almost as small as her voice. She was sitting, but I could tell she was about five-five, and probably didn't even weigh a hundred pounds. She had bumps and curves in all the right places, but scaled down. A pixie-like face with bright blue eyes was framed by flame red hair in a page boy cut.

I showed her my ID. "I'm looking into these threats you ladies have been getting," I said.

"I haven't been called," she said. Her voice had a note of disappointment in it. I guess she hated being left out.

"Do you think it's serious?"

"Shoot, I don't know. I guess it could be, but why would anybody wanna do that?"

I made some notes. It was curious that she hadn't been called, but that could just have been because whoever was doing it hadn't gotten around to her. She didn't seem to know much, nor did she seem all that worried about it. In fact, I was getting a sense that none of them were really all that worried – maybe because they looked to me to solve the problem. I thanked her and popped across the hall to the last of the models, Michele Mignon.

Mignon was standing in the middle of the room when I entered, an enigmatic look on her pale face. Her jet black hair was combed straight down the sides of her narrow skull, ending at her shoulders. She was as tall as me, with narrow shoulders, flared hips, and long, shapely legs – all of which was on display under the dress, or shirt – I wasn't sure what to call what looked like a long t-shirt – she wore. The white fabric was translucent, and she wasn't wearing anything beneath it. I still hadn't gotten used to the casual way models displayed their bodies.

"So, Mr. Pennyback," she said. "You get to me. What do you want to know?"

She had a deep, slightly raspy voice, and when she talked to you, she stared right into your eyes.

"Have you received any threatening calls?" I asked. Not much sense beating about the bush with this one, I thought.

"Not yet, but it's just a matter of time."

"What makes you say that?"

She looked at me as if I'd just wet my pants, or tracked mud on her best carpet.

"If whoever this is really wants to hurt Calvin's business, they'll go after everyone. It just makes sense."

It made sense to me, too. I was surprised that it had occurred to her. Beautiful though they were, Calvin Rigg's models wouldn't win any academic competitions.

"If you get a threat, would it make you quit?" I asked.

She shook her head. Her hair swirled across her face, almost covering a wan smile. "Nah," she said. "I can't afford to be unemployed - and walking out on a top designer like Calvin would make people wonder about you, you know. You think you're gonna catch this creep?"

I hadn't thought about that. It would be a strong motivator for the models to ignore the threats. The caller didn't seem to understand the fashion business any more than I did. If not part of the business, why the effort to ruin Rigg?

"I'll do my best," I said.

I left her, and walked to the break room, a wide room at the back with a table, eight plain wooden chairs, a mid-sized refrigerator, a large coffee maker, a microwave, and a sink. There were plastic cups, ceramic mugs and small paper plates in the cabinet over the sink. Surprisingly, the place was clean, without the usual scattering of stale food, food wrappers, and dirty plates and cups, although it did smell of microwave popcorn and coffee. I sat at the table, took out my notebook, and began organizing what I'd learned so far.

It all fit on one page.

Name	called at/on	date called
B. Gunn	studio/phone	Jan. 23
G. Montand	studio/phone	Jan. 24
V. del Toro	studio/cell	Jan. 24
L.M. Tang	home/cell	Jan. 25
S. Kalishnakova	studio/phone	Jan. 26
J. Clooney	not called	
M. Mignon	not called	

C. Rigg called three times with demand for money (1 million)

Each time on studio landline

Perp using voice distorter

That was it. No discernible pattern, no motive, and not even one viable possible suspect. It was like looking for a needle in a pile of needles.

7.

After pocketing my notebook, I made my way back to the front. Cheney was still reading his newspaper, and the two seamstresses were hunched over their sewing machines. I entered the elevator and punched the button for the first floor.

At the second floor, the car stopped, and Jason Lane got on.

"Hey," he said. "Did you get to talk to everyone?" He looked down at the floor as he spoke, clutching a sheaf of papers tightly in his hands.

"Yeah, I did."

"Any ideas of who is doing this to Calvin?"

"Not a clue yet," I said. "But, it's early. I'll find out who it is – you can count on that."

He mumbled something. I looked sharply at him, causing him to step back against the wall of the elevator car. "It's a shame this is happening," he said. "Calvin's a good boss. He doesn't deserve this."

We did the rest of the ride in silence; me thinking about the lack of leads, and him looking down at the floor. He kept his eyes on his feet as we walked out and to the parking garage. He mumbled something else as we entered the garage. His car, a shiny canary yellow Jeep with black top, black hood, and black front grille, was in one of the slots near the entrance. He smiled shyly at me as he got in and put his papers on the passenger seat.

"Check you later," I said.

"Yeah, sure," he said.

The Jeep rumbled as he started it, belching smoke from the rear. He pulled out of the slot and, with a cloud of gray smoke trailing him, drove off. I found my car where I'd left it in the rear of the bay, got in and headed to the office.

Heather looked up from her work, smiling, as I walked into the office.

"Well, did you enjoy your morning with all those beautiful models?" she asked.

I ignored her question. Taking the notebook from my pocket, I tore out the page with my notes on it and tossed it onto her desk.

"How about checking out these times for me, honey bunch," I said. "See if you can find some kind of pattern in the calls."

She frowned down at the paper, and then looked back up at me.

"What am I supposed to be looking for?"

"Darned if I know, really. I can't figure this thing out. After talking to everyone at Rigg's studio, threatening the models is making less and less sense to me. None of them seem scared enough to quit, and from what I learned today, even if they did, he could replace them much easier than they could get new jobs."

She picked the paper up. After reading it carefully, she smiled.

"You know," she said. "Maybe whoever this is isn't trying to drive him out of business."

"Then, what is he – or she – trying to do?"

She tapped Rigg's name on the paper. "You wrote here that he was called and asked for a million dollars. Maybe that's what this is really all about and the calls to the models are just misdirection."

"Or," I said. "Maybe they're an extra

incentive to get him to pay the money."

"Of course," she said. "He might not *have* that kind of money."

"Or, he has it, and paying it will drive him out of business."

I laughed.

"What's so funny, boss?"

"We sound like the two seamstresses that work for Rigg. They're a couple of strange, but nice, old ladies who're always finishing each other's sentences."

"Is that a good thing, or a bad thing?" she asked. Her brow was furrowed.

"Neither good, nor bad – it's just what happens when two people have spent so much time with each other they're able to get inside each other's minds."

She shook her head. "Now, that is *not* a good thing. I don't know if I want you inside my head, and I certainly *don't* want to be inside that head of yours. Your thought processes are just too strange."

"Oh, come on, there's nothing strange about it. You and I have been working together for a long time now, it's perfectly natural."

Heather came to work for me shortly after I started the firm. When I discovered that paperwork was not my strong suit, I put an ad in the paper for an administrative assistant. She'd just graduated from secretarial school and was looking for a job. I couldn't pay her much at first, but she didn't seem to mind, and over time, as I discovered just how valuable she was – especially her ability with computers – I gradually raised her salary. Since she'd gotten her PI license the year before, she was no longer my employee, but my partner. I'd wanted to change the name of A.E. Pennyback, Confidential Enquiries to reflect that, but she argued against it. Just as well. It would have meant getting new letterhead and invoices printed, and even with the ten thousand a month retainer the firm of Holcombe, Stein and Chang paid us, we weren't exactly rolling in cash. More often than not, after expenses – including Heather's salary – were paid, I didn't pay myself, so we'd have cash in the bank for unforeseen emergencies.

In more than a decade of working together, despite being totally different personalities, we had learned to anticipate each other. We didn't often complete each other's sentences, but we didn't often *have* to speak to communicate.

"It might be natural," she said. "But, it doesn't mean I have to like it."

8.

For the rest of the day, I let Heather stew over the fact that we were inside each other's minds.

I tucked myself into my office and huddled behind my desk, trying to make sense of the case.

The problem was – nothing about the case was making any sense.

I took it as a given that someone had it in for Calvin Rigg – which might or might not be true, but I had to start with *something*. There was always the possibility that one of the models could be the real target, and the threats against the others were meant to hide that fact, but the attempt to extort money from Rigg made that unlikely. So, I had to try and determine who wanted to hurt Rigg – either by running him out of business, or out of money. Unlike his former partner, Franklin Honeywell, who almost everyone had hated, and who he had been accused of killing, Rigg was, as far as I could determine, a popular figure. I had yet to talk to his main competitors, but Heather had found no indications from her computer searches that there had been any feuds going, or any gossip about bad blood between Rigg and any of the other designers.

There you have it – I had a big bunch of nothing to work with. No suspects, no real leads, no motives – no nothing.

I was sitting there, leaning back in my chair contemplating the spider web cracks in the ceiling, when the phone buzzed. I pressed the little red button. "Yeah, what is it?" I asked.

"Quincy on the line for you, boss," Heather said. The note of displeasure that had been in her voice was gone. "He says it's important."

"Okay, put him through." As if I had a choice in the matter.

Ten thousand bucks a month buys Quincy my time whenever he wants it. That and the fact that he and I have been friends for a long time – all the way back to my army days, when I was assigned to a Special Operations unit at Ft. Bragg, North Carolina and he'd been one of the fort's Judge Advocate General lawyers.

"Hey, Al," he said when Heather put him through. "Did I catch you at a bad time?"

"Not really, amigo," I said. "What can I do for you?"

There was a long pause. This was unusual. Quincy normally plowed right into whatever his subject was – one of his strong points as a trial lawyer when he was a JAG. I heard a throat clearing sound.

"Uh, it's not something I want to talk about over an open line, Al," he said finally. "Can you come by the office first thing tomorrow?"

I told him I could, but after I broke the connection I had two puzzles buzzing around in my head.

On Tuesday morning, I called Heather from home to let her know I'd be late getting to the office. Sandra and I had a leisurely breakfast, and after she went off to school, I took my time cleaning the kitchen. I waited until after nine to head for Quincy's office to avoid the morning traffic.

The offices of Holcombe, Stein and Chang are located in one of the many steel and glass towers lining K Street, north of the White House and in close proximity to the Congress. It's here that most of the highest powered lobbyists in DC have their headquarters, and from here that they dispense the cash that often controls politics in this country. Quincy's firm didn't do lobbying, but they represented some of the outfits that did – the reason they were able to pay me such a large monthly retainer. To their credit, though, they did a lot of *pro bono* work for people who couldn't afford their six hundred bucks an hour fees.

I parked in the building's basement garage, pocketing the ticket so that Quincy's assistant could stamp it to keep me from having to pay the fifty dollar parking fee, and took the elevator up to the ground floor.

The elevator from the garage was near the front of the large reception area. At the center, and about halfway to a large wall that blocked the center three-fourths of the space, was a long, chest-high desk behind which sat four women in forest green coats. I approached the one on the far right, a broad shouldered, large breasted woman who looked at me with a smile on her dark brown face, but wariness in her dark brown eyes. As she leaned forward to take my ID I could see the butt of the revolver strapped to her ample waist. Security had been upgraded since my last visit.

The wariness was gone from her eyes as she slid my ID back across the desk.

"Mr. Pennyback," she said. "You're on the access list for Holcombe, Stein and Chang. I assume you know the way to the elevators?"

I did. I nodded and smiled as I pocketed my ID. Her smile brightened.

I walked around the desk to the right, past the wall, behind which was a bank of six elevators. I entered the rightmost car and punched the button for the twelfth floor. The doors slid silently shut, and the car started up immediately with enough acceleration to cause me to feel the downward drag as gravity pulled at my body. They'd upgraded the elevators as well.

The ride up was swift and silent. The doors slid open onto the law firm's reception area. No real changes there. Same receptionist sitting at the same desk in front of the elevator, who favored me with the same bright smile as I exited the elevator. She motioned me past to her right. I know the way. A long, wide hallway past closed doors behind which associates toil away researching cases or preparing briefs for which clients will be charged a hefty hourly fee, much of which those associates will never see. But, they still make more a year than I do, so I have little sympathy for them.

Quincy Chang, a partner in the firm since he left the army, has a corner office with a view of the Capitol Rotunda. His partners' offices have a similar view, and according to him, are larger. You could play field hockey in his office, so I imagine they need maps to find their way around theirs.

His secretary, a woman of indeterminate age who guards his door as if his office contained the crown jewels, sat behind her desk as usual. As usual, she batted her phony eyelashes at me and arched her back to cause her breasts to jut against her blouse. Her hair, usually gray or bluish in color, had been dyed a bright red and she had it done up in a style from the fifties – curly and fluffy in front and pulled tight in back. She was probably a real doll in her youth, and she liked to remind me of it every time I came to see her boss. I winked at her and said that when Sandra dumped me I'd come calling. She blew me a kiss and told me to go on in.

Quincy was sitting behind a desk larger than a pool table with a manila folder open in front of him. He was in shirt sleeves. He looked up as I entered.

"Hey, Al," he said. "Thanks for coming.

Would you like a cup of coffee?"

He motioned at the coffee maker on the credenza to his right. He already had a mugful on his desk at his elbow. The smell of freshly brewed coffee was thick in the air. Three identical mugs sat next to the urn. I poured myself one and returned to the chair at the side of his desk.

"What's so important and secret you couldn't talk about it on the phone?" I asked. I took a sip. It was Jamaican. Tasted like it had been made from freshly ground beans.

He tapped the folder. "Consolidated Insurance is one of our biggest clients," he said. "They have a problem that requires delicate handling and the utmost privacy. Just a precaution that bit about the phone, but you never know."

"What is it – an employee stealing or something? Why don't they just call the cops?"

"No, it's not that. It's one of their policyholders. They've received a claim that they fear might be bogus."

"I thought these big insurance companies had in-house claims adjustors who can investigate these things. Why don't they just deny the claim?"

"It's not that simple." He shook his head,

looking down at the several sheets of paper in the folder. "The policyholder is a wealthy local businessman with some pretty high level connections with members of congress and in government. If they deny the claim outright, he's likely to take them to court. If one of their in-house investigators starts snooping around, he might also make trouble for them. They're hoping you could do it discretely without linking it back to them."

"And, how in hell am I supposed to do that?"

He held up his hands in supplication. "Hell, Al," he said. "I don't know. You have this uncanny ability to do things that seem beyond the ability of ordinary people. I was hoping you'd come up with something. Otherwise, Consolidated is out a two million dollar payment."

I took a deep breath. "Two million dollars? What the hell could this guy have insured that's worth that much money?"

He took a sheet from the thin stack and handed it to me. It was a copy of the insurance claim form. The claimant was Wilmont Haverford, at a residence in McLean, Virginia just off Chain Bridge Road. The claimed amount was two million dollars for stolen and damaged property. The stolen items were listed as four original oil paintings. I didn't recognize the artists, but the individual value of each painting was over three hundred thousand. The eight hundred grand for damages was for five Ming Dynasty vases that were smashed. I whistled.

"You see what I mean?" Quincy said. "And the missing and damaged items were just a small part of this guy's total art collection."

"He reported it to the police, of course?"

"Yeah," he said, handing me a copy of the police report which was submitted with the claim.

According to the police report, Haverford, and his wife Cynthia, had gone out to dinner on January 24th. They returned home around midnight to find that someone had broken into their house. They immediately called the cops. The detective investigating the incident confirmed that a rear door window had been smashed, and listed the damages he'd seen. The crime scene technician found no fingerprints or other forensic evidence that might help identify the perpetrator or perpetrators, which meant the incident would in all likelihood end up in the cold case files – forever unsolved unless one of the missing paintings turned up somewhere. At the bottom of the report, the detective noted that there'd been an electrical outage in the neighborhood around 9 pm, which lasted for thirty minutes, causing the Haverford's alarm system to shut off. Quincy handed me another sheet of paper – a report from Securitech, the company responsible for the alarm system. When the power went off, Securitech had sent a mobile patrol to the area, but had seen no suspicious vehicles or anything else amiss.

"Not much here to go on," I said. "Sounds to me like a burglar just took advantage of the power outage. Anyone else in the neighborhood report break-ins during that period?"

"No, and that's what triggered the alarms for Consolidated," Quincy said. "Haverford's not the only person in that particular neighborhood with valuables. You'd think there would have been other hits. At any rate, they just want to make sure before they shell out that kind of money."

I ran it through my mind. I couldn't very well refuse the assignment, but Quincy wasn't giving me much to work with. I would need to find a way to look into it without involving the insurance company – not an easy task. Then, I had a thought.

"Other than sending a patrol around, what did the security company do?" I asked.

He shuffled through the papers. "They sent a team out to check the alarm system the day after the incident," he said. "Other than having to reset it and get Haverford to set a new PIN, they found nothing wrong with it. Why do you ask?"

"I can't pose as an insurance investigator," I said. "And, pretending to be a cop wouldn't work either – not to mention it could get me busted and my license yanked – so, I'm thinking I'll go in as a customer service rep of the security company. You know, follow up on the service call to make sure the customer's satisfied."

"I knew you'd come up with some crazy idea," he said. He laughed. "The real crazy thing is – it just might work."

I certainly hoped so.

9.

After leaving Quincy's office, I called my friend Carlton Raine, a retired CIA agent who lived in a fortified log cabin in the woods just beyond my farm. As I'd anticipated, he saw no problem in getting me documents that would identify me as an employee of Securitech. He promised to have them by the end of the day. He invited Sandra and me to join him and his girlfriend Elizabeth Sung for dinner - and between dessert and coffee presented me with a photo ID in the name of Paul Johnson – not a name I would have chosen myself, but since I was only using it once, it didn't matter - and a page of information about Securitech, just in case Haverford asked any questions. I didn't ask him where he'd gotten the photo of me for the ID. There are some things that Raine can do that it's best not knowing too much about.

As I pocketed the ID, Raine laid a hand on my arm. "I've a feeling you've never done this type of undercover job before, son," he said.

He had a way of knowing things that was uncanny.

"You're right," I said. "But, how hard can it be?"

"It's not, but you have to keep it simple. Remember, the key is to get the mark or suspect talking. Don't say anything you don't absolutely have to say, and ask lots of questions."

"Won't that make him suspicious?"

He laughed. "Not if your questions let him show off how much he knows," he said. "You're there to get his views on the company's service, so stress that. You'll want to gently nudge him into telling you what he thinks went wrong with the system. Listen carefully, and if he's up to no good, he'll tell you."

"Yeah, like he'll just confess that his claim is bogus?"

"Not directly, but listen to what he says, and what he doesn't say. Sometimes, the topics he tries to avoid will tell you more than what he actually says."

I processed his advice. It made sense. In a

way, it was a variation on a suspect interview. Get the suspect talking, make him comfortable, and listen. Watch his reaction to questions. His body language will often tell you more than his words. It was a challenge, but I felt that I was up to it.

I left home for the office early the next morning, beating Sandra out of the house by thirty minutes, which left her to clean the breakfast dishes. I was early enough to beat the morning rush hour traffic, but still didn't make it in before Heather.

She was sitting at her desk, sipping tea and reading the early edition of the *Washington Post*.

"I thought you got all your news from the Internet," I said as I shucked my coat.

"I like to read the paper sometimes to compare its coverage with what's on the net," she said, making a face at me. "What did Quincy want with you yesterday?"

I gave her the rundown on the insurance job.

"It shouldn't take me more than a day or two to knock this off," I said. "Then, we can get back to finding out who is threatening Calvin Rigg."

"No rush there. I'm still compiling dossiers on all the models and other staff at his studio. So far, I haven't seen anything interesting."

"What about his main competitors?"

"Not much there," she said. "His closest competition is Samuel Dyson, and everything I've found indicates that the two of them are still good friends."

I left her still reading the paper and went into my office. I'd decided to call Wilmont Haverford and make an appointment to meet with him at his residence. Securitech had offices in DC and Virginia, so I decided to call from the office phone just in case he had Caller ID. My cell phone is a 301 exchange, which is one of the Maryland area codes, and that might arouse his suspicions.

I dialed the number he'd put on the insurance claim form. He answered after three rings.

"Haverford here," a deep voice said. "How can I help you?"

"Mr. Haverford, Paul Johnson with Securitech," I said. "I'm calling in regard to the recent home security incident you experienced."

"Your people already came and fixed the system." There was a petulant note in his voice.

"I'm aware of that, sir," I said patiently. "We want to make sure, though, that our customers are completely satisfied. It's my job to check their work and to find out if you have any other questions or issues."

There was a long pause. "I see," he said. "So, you'll need to come to the house?"

"Yes, to take a look at what they did. If it's no inconvenience, I'd like to ask you a few questions, and if I could do it all in one visit, it would be great."

Another pause. "I suppose that's okay. When would you like to do it?"

"Any time that's convenient to you, sir," I said, trying to sound like a vendor anxious to please a customer, but hoping he would want to get it over with as quickly as possible.

"I can be home at ten," he said. "Can you make it then?"

Damn straight I could. I agreed to meet him at his house at ten. He offered directions, but I told him I knew how to get there. It wouldn't have been logical for me not to know since I was supposed to be part of the company protecting his place. I'd have Heather do an Internet map search which would not only pinpoint his address, but give me directions from the office.

With two printed sheets in hand, one with street-by-street directions, the other with a street map with his house marked with a star, I set out for McLean at 9:20. I went up Fourth Street to M, and then left and around to Maine Avenue. At Independence Avenue I hooked a left, and then cut around the Lincoln Memorial over to Constitution, and then left across the Roosevelt Memorial Bridge, taking the George Washington Parkway exit toward the west. Chain Bridge Road, Virginia Route 123, which goes past the public entrance of the Central Intelligence Agency, is about eight miles, and at that time of morning, the drive was quicker than the three mile drive from my office. Traffic was light on Chain Bridge Road. I had the directions on the passenger seat, consulting them frequently as I drove past the CIA complex, but also keeping an eye out for the drivers who insisted on cutting in front of traffic without signaling.

Haverford's house wasn't actually on Chain Bridge Road. It was on a narrow street off to the right, just before Old Dominion Drive – a slightly hilly neighborhood of colonial style mansions set among towering hardwood trees and surrounded by black iron fences with fancy gates. Haverford's house would have been invisible from the street if the trees hadn't been bare. The three story red brick colonial with a large portico entrance stood like a medieval castle among the gnarled trees. From the street, a cobblestone drive went up and curved around under the portico. Off to the right was a rectangular cobblestone area for parking, and beyond that a detached four-car garage. I pulled into the parking area.

The doorbell was a deep, rolling chime, like something from a monster movie, and had me expecting a tall, pale butler with a strange accent. Instead, the double doors were opened by a tiny, pale woman with snow white hair.

"Yes?" she asked, with a slight southern drawl. "Can I help you?"

I showed her the Johnson ID. "I have an appointment with Mr. Haverford."

She stepped aside to let me enter, and then led me toward an arched opening into a large room that from the number of chairs and small tables was used for receptions. You could have played a game of football in it. At the rear was a glass wall that looked out on a manicured garden dotted with statues. Expensive looking paintings dotted the walls, and large green and blue vases sat in every corner. There were large doors to the right and left.

From the left I heard the sound of glass

breaking. The little woman stopped. "Just a moment, please," she said nervously. "I'll see if Mr. Haverford is available."

She disappeared through the door. A few minutes later, she peeked around the door and motioned me forward.

The room I entered looked like a museum. Expensive looking paintings and prints hung on the dark wooden walls, and display shelves and tables held small statues of ivory, jade and other stone, along with urns and vases in ceramic and metal – the golden metal vases were probably gold, but I'm no expert – many with stones inlaid in the surface. On the wall to the right, there was a large blank space, which I assumed was where the stolen paintings had once hung.

A man of about my height and weight, with sandy brown hair and a florid complexion, dressed in a gray suit, faced a woman about six inches shorter, with lank blonde hair, too much makeup, and anger on her face, who stood on the other side of the waist high display table, her hands on her ample hips and her breasts heaving. On the floor at their feet was a scattering of green porcelain shards that, from the looks on their faces had once been an expensive piece of pottery.

"You did that deliberately," the man said

through clinched teeth.

"Prove it," she said.

I made a throat clearing sound. They both turned to face me. The man took a deep breath. The woman glared at me.

"You're Johnson from Securitech?" the man asked.

I flashed my fake ID. "That's right," I said. "You're Mr. Haverford?"

He gave the ID a quick glance. "Yes, and the clum-, er, this is my wife."

I nodded at her. She continued to glare.

"If this is a bad time, I can come back later," I said.

"No," he said. "Let's get this over with. You want to check the system first, or ask your questions?"

The guy was playing right into my hands. I could ask my questions, do a cursory check of the system, and get the hell out of there.

"Why don't we get the questions out of the way," I said.

Cynthia Haverford switched her glare from me to her husband. "Why are we answering *his* questions for Christ's sake? It was his company's equipment that failed and let the turds in here to destroy my precious vases and steal my paintings."

"Your *precious* vases were pieces of shit, my dear, and the paintings were not yours – they were mine."

She stamped a foot, sending a shard of porcelain skittering across the floor. "My Ming vases were priceless – far more valuable than this stupid thing was." She pointed down at the pieces on the floor.

Haverford's cheeks turned redder, and he clenched his fists. "That *stupid* thing was a Celadon vase from Korea's Silla Dynasty, and one of the finest specimens of its kind."

This was easier than I'd thought it would be. All I had to do was let them talk.

Cynthia Haverford was at the point of tears now. "I should never have married you, Wilmont. You're cruel. I'm glad we're getting a divorce."

"I can't say that I'm unhappy about it either," he shot back. "Now, if you'd just be reasonable about the settlement, we could get on with our lives."

"If *I* would be reasonable? Why, why . . . you weasel, it's you that's being unreasonable."

He moved forward, his shoes crunching

on the broken vase, and leaned over, bracing himself on the stand. "I have offered you half of everything. What more could you want?"

"You know that all I wanted was those four paintings and my vases. Why did they have to be what was taken? Why?" That last word was uttered in a plaintive cry.

"Look, Cynthia," he said. "You'll get half the money from the insurance settlement. You can use that to replace the damn vases. They weren't all that rare."

"What about the paintings?"

"Well, that's just tough luck," he said. "Don't forget, I loved those paintings as much as you did." He then blinked and looked at me. "I'm sorry, Mr. Johnson . . . you had some questions for me about the incident?"

"Yes, as a matter of fact," I said. "When the technicians reset the system, did they tell you why the battery power didn't kick in when the house power went off?"

He blinked again. "Uh . . . yes . . . it seems that the connection to the backup power was broken. A loose wire or something. They fixed it."

"Any idea how it got loosened?"

"The guy said it could have worked loose – especially if it wasn't on tight enough when the system was installed."

Funny, I thought, that it would work loose just when the electricity went off. Of course, that was no proof that the guy had faked the claim.

"I understand the house was empty at the time?"

"Yes," he said. "My wife and I were out to dinner."

"And, the paintings were the only things taken? Were they cut from the frames?"

"Yes," Cynthia Haverford said. "The paintings were the *only* things missing. And, they took them frames and all."

"The frames are worth several hundred dollars each," her husband added.

"Four large paintings in the frames would have been too much for one person," I said. "There had to be more than one thief. They would also have had to have a vehicle to move them. I wonder why our patrol didn't spot anything."

"We're the only house on this block protected by Securitech," he said. "So, they only cruised our street. The thieves probably had a van or truck in one of the nearby service roads. Your patrol wouldn't have gone down any of them."

I nodded. He was right, of course. It *could* have gone down that way. But, I had my doubts. I couldn't think of any more questions, though, without arousing their suspicions.

"Yeah, you're right," I said. "Look, please accept our company's apologies for any inconvenience. Now, if you don't mind, I'd like to look at the control panel."

"Sure," he said. "Lily, our housekeeper, can show you where it is." He went to the door. "Oh, Lily, would you please show Mr. Johnson the alarm control box?"

The tiny woman came into the room, nodded, and motioned me to follow her.

We went across the reception room to the door on that side, which led into a large dining room. Through that, we went into the kitchen, a room as large as the kitchen in some big restaurants. The alarm control panel was just inside the rear door, a large green box mounted head high on the wall.

I opened the cover and peered around the insides as if I knew what I was doing.

"So, Lily, I take it you're not live-in help?"

"No," she said. "I come in five days a week – mostly to do cleaning and laundry."

"There's no cook?"

"Well, before Mr. and Mrs. Haverford started having their problems, they ate out a lot. When they did eat at home, she'd hire a cook part time."

"They're having problems?" I asked innocently.

"You didn't notice how they are with each other? Been fighting like cats and dogs for the past few months. She finally said she couldn't take it anymore and asked for a divorce. Now, they argue over who gets what. I think he doesn't want to go through with it, though. That's why they were out that night. He was trying to talk her out of the divorce. Didn't work, though."

"So, they're splitting everything down the middle?"

She laughed. "Not so's you'd know it. They each have their favorite things, and it really gets messy when they both like the same thing. I swear, these two are like little kids sometimes."

Her face turned red. I think she'd realized that she was spilling family secrets to a total stranger. She clamped her lips shut and looked down at her feet. I'd heard enough, though. I was convinced that Haverford had faked his claim, and thought I knew *why* he'd done it. All I had to do now was prove *how* he'd done it.

10.

I broke off my conversation with the housekeeper, thanked her for her time, and left the Haverfords to their domestic discord. It was nearly noon, so I drove into McLean and had a lunch of curried chicken at Absolute Thai, a restaurant on the second floor of a little shopping center not far from the center of town.

After washing lunch down with a bottle of *Singha* beer, I drove back to the office.

Heather was sitting at her computer looking glumly at the screen when I walked in.

"The ether not giving up its secrets today?" I asked.

"I'm having a hard time getting anything solid on anyone at Calvin's studio except him," she said. "He's all over the news with the way his designs have been gaining popularity. But, the others are little more than blurry figures in the news photos."

"Maybe you need to take a break from it," I said. "I have a name I'd like you to run a check on." I gave her Wilmont and Cynthia Haverford's names. "See what you can find on these two."

"Anything in particular?"

"No, just dig up whatever's available," I said. "I think this guy has filed a bogus insurance claim, but I need something that might help prove it."

She turned back to her computer and tapped on the keyboard. Almost immediately her eyes lit up and her lips turned up in a smile. Whatever she'd been looking for must have come up in the first batch. As long as she was happy, I wasn't unhappy. I went to my office.

Slumped in my chair, I stared at the blank gray screen of my computer. I took my notebook out of my pocket and put it on the desk next to the keyboard. I then reached into the left desk drawer and took out a new notebook, which I flipped open and put next to the first one. I opened the first notebook to the last page of entries – my list of the models' names and when they received threats. On the blank page of the new notebook I wrote *Haverford vs Consolidated Insurance.* Beneath that I began noting what I knew or had observed about the case.

> *Haverfords getting divorce*
> *Dispute over division of property*
> *Both wanted missing paintings*
> *Backup power on alarm failed at same time as power failure*
> *Four missing paintings too large for one person to carry*
> *Securitech patrol saw no suspicious vehicle*

That was all I had – or all that I could think of. Not a lot to go on, but I was still convinced that Haverford was pulling a con on the insurance company. The backup power failing at the same time as the main power was too much of a coincidence, and I don't believe in coincidences. I looked again at the sixth entry. 'No suspicious vehicles' could mean a lot of things, but I guessed it meant the patrol hadn't seen any vehicles they wouldn't expect to see in the area. That, however, left a lot of vehicles that could move four stolen paintings – from a power company van to a soccer mom's car.

I picked up the phone and dialed Quincy.

His secretary put me through

immediately.

"Al," he said. "Anything on the insurance case?"

"I think Haverford is cheating the company," I said. "But, I haven't found a way to prove it yet. You might be able to help."

"If it saves a client two million bucks, of course I'll help. What do you need?"

I asked him to check with Securitech about their patrol's observations. He promised to get back to me as quickly as he could. It was late in the day, and I was anxious to get home, so I told him to call me back the next morning.

I looked at the two notebooks. No brilliant flashes of inspiration. Just my crabby handwriting sitting there staring up at me. In one case I had a bad act, but no actor that I could point to. In the other, a bad actor, but no way yet to prove how he'd done the dirty deed. It would be nice, I thought, if I had a computer that would crunch all the facts I had and tell me which ones were useful. Unfortunately, a computer is just a dumb machine that's incredibly fast in amassing, and even sorting, data. It takes nature's own computer, the human brain, to make sense of information. A computer, for instance, can't tell the difference between a *false* fact and a *true* fact, or when someone is telling a lie.

Unfortunately, my brain was at a loss.

When that happens, I find the only useful thing to do is go home and find something else to think about – like taking Sandra out for a big Korean barbecue dinner, and then going back home for an extended period of bedroom gymnastics.

The next morning, refreshed, the two of us did our usual morning routine – four miles through the forest behind the farm, thirty minutes of pounding the heavy bag in the barn, followed by thirty minutes of meditation for me while Sandra showered. She did breakfast while I showered, and we ate together at the rickety wooden table next to the stove while we listened to the early morning news on the local National Public Radio station.

I managed to keep my mind off both cases until I walked into the office. Sandra sat there with a look of smug satisfaction on her face, a cup of tea in her hand, and an open notebook at her elbow.

"I have some interesting information about your insurance case," she said.

"Can it wait until I get my second cup of coffee?"

Even though Heather seldom drinks

coffee, she often brews a pot – partly for me, and partly for the occasional visitor. I walked over and poured a mug, sipping as I walked back to her desk.

"Can I tell you now?" she asked.

I took another sip, letting the rich, woody aroma caress my nostrils, and enjoying the warmth as it crossed my tongue and slid down my throat. I took a deep breath.

"Okay, shoot," I said.

"Well, for starters, the Haverfords are in the midst of a rather messy divorce," she said. I didn't want to burst her bubble by telling her that I already knew that, so I just nodded for her to continue. "Their public spats over who gets what are so bad they've even made the gossip columns."

"Interesting, but what does that have to do with their insurance claim?"

She gave me a petulant look. "How should I know? You told me to look up everything on them, and that's what I did. Now, do you want to hear the rest of it?"

Heather hates to be interrupted when she's on an information roll. I looked appropriately chastened and nodded again. "Sorry," I said. "Go ahead."

"Wilmont Haverford is as rich as Croesus

according to the reports I found. He owns several companies, mostly construction firms, doing work for the government. He also has a company that does electrical installations for some of the army bases in the area, and he has controlling interest in two banks. The guy's net worth is over thirty million dollars. Hardly the profile of someone who would try to defraud an insurance company, don't you think?"

"He certainly doesn't sound like he needs the money . . . wait . . . you said he owns a company that does electrical work?"

She looked down at her notebook. "Yeah – ElectroCity – according to the records, they install generators and do general work on the power plants at the military bases. Why?"

A thought was forming in my mind. "I take it ElectroCity has utility vans?"

"Duh," she said. "What kind of electrical company doesn't have vans?"

"Hang on a minute," I said. I picked up her phone and dialed Quincy. "Quince," I said when his secretary connected him. "Did you check with Securitech yet?"

"Yeah, I did," he answered. "I was just about to call you."

"Did they recall seeing an ElectroCity van in the area that night?"

"As a matter of fact, they did," he said. "But, it belongs to Haverford's company and is often there, so they thought nothing of it."

The *how* of Haverford's scam fell neatly into place. "I think, though, that Consolidated Insurance will be interested. That van explains how he pulled off the robbery of his own home."

"You care to explain it to me?" I detected a note of skepticism in his voice.

Oh, ye of little faith, I thought. It was really simple when you thought about it. I described how I thought – no, how I was *certain* – Haverford had pulled it off.

He'd hired a crew from ElectroCity to short out the neighborhood power – a simple task for any competent electrician, and even simpler for someone experienced in doing major power systems. In the meantime, someone else was stationed at the house to disable the alarm system's backup power. Once that was done, the perpetrators simply went inside and took their time robbing and trashing the place. When the coast was clear, they moved the stolen paintings to the company van. The stolen goods were probably stashed somewhere on company property.

"Did the power company find out what caused the power outage?" I asked.

"Sure, some debris got into one of their switching stations and shorted it out. Once they located it, they fixed it in a few minutes and restored power."

Sweet, I thought. Short the local power with debris. It happens a lot during the winter, so it wouldn't arouse any suspicions.

"I think if you check the whereabouts of ElectroCity's vans and crews, you'll find one was out at that time, and I'll bet dollars to donuts it'll be the one Securitech saw. If you can find them, you should be able to sweat the truth out of them."

"Okay," he said. "That makes sense. But, why would Haverford do it?"

"He and his wife are involved in a nasty dispute over property division. If you'd ever seen the two of them together, you'd understand," I said. "The four stolen paintings just happen to be items they both want, while the damaged vases were *her* favorites. My guess is he planned to split the insurance money with her and keep the paintings for himself – grudgingly. If he could find a way to screw her out of the cash, I bet he'd do that as well."

I heard him chuckle over the line. "Wow, who would have thought a man his age could act like that – and, with his money, too."

"Both of them act like spoiled brats. I'll bet if the wife could have figured a way to do it to him, she would have. Anyway, I should think the insurance company can handle it from here."

"That they can, amigo," he said. "Oh, and by the way, they're paying ten percent of the saved claim, so that's a cool two hundred thousand in your bank account."

I was smiling broadly when I broke the connection.

"You look like the cat about to eat the canary," Heather said.

"More like the cat who's about to deposit two hundred grand in our bank account," I said.

Her eyes widened. "That much for a day's work? And, you didn't even get shot at or have to beat up anyone."

"Speaking of beating people up, we'd better get back on Calvin Rigg's case. I think I'll drop by his studio and see if there's anything new. You feel up to hitting the research grind again?"

She didn't bother answering. A payday like we'd just been promised is a powerful motivator. She swiveled around in her chair, and her fingers fairly flew over her keyboard.

Even the crosstown traffic was cooperative. I made it from my place to Rigg's studio in record time – and scored a parking slot on the first level in front of the parking garage to boot.

Smiles are contagious. I was grinning when I entered the lobby and approached the receptionist, who took it for flirting, and simpered back at me as she waved me to the elevators. As the elevator inched upward, I pinched myself as a reminder not to think mornings like this would happen more than once in a long, long time. It didn't work. I was still smiling when the doors slid open on the second floor.

The scene in Rigg's reception area was of a mood that was the polar opposite of my own, and it wiped most of the smile off my face.

Everyone, including the janitor, was standing around with hangdog looks on their faces. Lisa Farnsworth, her brown face streaked with tears, was being consoled by a crying Tillie Moyer and a dour looking Greg Cheney. The models, still dressed in the tacky outfits they wore when not working, stood in a clump murmuring to each other. The janitor, Caleb Billings, his eyes red, stood off to himself in a corner staring at the wall. Calvin Rigg, a look of utter devastation on his face, stood near the desk. Jason Lane, looking confused, stood at his side. Except for Farnsworth, who kept her head buried in Moyer's hair, everyone's gazed turned to me as I stepped out of the elevator.

I was about to ask 'who died,' when I noticed that one person was missing. I didn't see Martha Frank, Lisa Farnsworth's other half. I bit back what would have been a stupid and inappropriate comment.

"What's going on?" I asked as I approached Rigg.

It took him a few seconds to compose himself. "It's Martha . . . she . . .," he had trouble forming the words. "She was . . . late . . . and she's . . . never late to work."

He then broke down and started sobbing. I looked at Jason Lane.

"When Martha didn't come to work at her usual time," he said crisply. "I called her house, but got no answer. It's not like her to take off without notifying me, so I called the police. They went to her house, and found her dead. She'd apparently fallen asleep with a gas heater on, and somehow the flame died. The police just called us back a few minutes ago with the news. They found an empty vodka bottle on the floor near her chair, and a glass at her feet. They figure she drank a bit too much and fell asleep. A draft must have blown the heater flame out."

I put a hand on Rigg's shoulder. "I'm sorry, Calvin," I said. "I know this must hit you hard."

He dabbed at his eyes with his fingers, and took a deep breath. "Yeah, Martha has been with me a long time. She, Lisa and Stella were my first fulltime employees after the mess with Franklin ended. We were like a family."

"Will this interfere with your preparations for the next show?"

He shook his head. "It'll be difficult, but I think we can do it. I still remember how to cut fabric, and while I'm not as deft as Martha or Lisa, I can do it in a pinch. You have anything more on who it is that's threatening me?"

"I wish I could say yes," I said, shaking my head. "But, not yet. Don't you worry, though. I *will* find out who it is."

"I know you will." He smiled wanly. "I haven't forgotten how you proved the impossible when I was accused of murder. Was there anything else you needed to talk to anyone about?"

"Nothing that can't wait," I said. "I'll get out of here and let you folks do what you have to do."

They were still consoling each other as the

elevator doors slid shut in my face. The day had now become what was more normal in the life of a private investigator.

11.

In the parking garage, I took out my notebook and made a note of Martha Frank's death – accidental? – I was taking nothing for granted in this case. When you have no suspects and no motive, everything is suspicious, and everyone is a potential suspect. Well, everyone but Martha Frank, that is.

When I got back to the office, Heather was sitting at her desk, sipping tea, and for a change, not peering at her computer screen.

"Is your computer down?" I asked.

"No," she said. "I'm just giving it a break. It's been working overtime today. I have a ton of information for you."

She took out a notebook, flipping it open. The pages were filled with her precise handwriting.

"Maybe you should sit down, or better yet, let's go into your office. There's a lot of stuff here for that brain of yours to process."

"Why don't we use my office?" I always felt better on home turf, and the front part of the office belonged totally to Heather.

She grabbed her notebook and followed me in, pulling the visitor's chair around to the side and putting her notebook on the edge of my desk. She opened it again.

"Okay," she said. "I only focused on information that might have a bearing on the threats – things that make people vulnerable, or grudges they might have against Calvin. It's surprising what's in some of their backgrounds." She then gave it to me person by person, starting with the models.

Bibi Gunn had a child out of wedlock when she was seventeen. Her parents had kicked her out, and she'd spent a few years on the street hooking before being spotted by Franklin Honeywell and hired as a model.

Genvieve Montand had been arrested for drug possession three times as a teenager, but had been put on probation. There was no record of any further arrests or drug use since she began modeling.

Svetlana Kalishnakova didn't have a

criminal record, but there were indications that she might have entered the U.S. illegally.

Michelle Mignon had a conviction for shoplifting.

Li Ming Tang was a former heroin addict, who had spent over a year in a rehab clinic when she was twenty-three.

Heather could find no records of any criminal activity or antisocial behavior by Jessica Clooney and Victoria del Toro.

Greg Cheney, the makeup man, had been arrested for assault, but given probation. He'd busted the jaw of a fellow makeup artist who had insulted his work at a fashion show five years earlier.

Caleb Billings the janitor was an Air Force veteran who had been medically discharged for alcoholism twenty years earlier. He'd had a string of menial jobs since, and had been hired by Rigg when he himself got out of jail after being cleared for the murder of his former partner.

Tillie Moyer the receptionist was, like Heather, a secretarial school graduate, hired by Rigg at the same time as Billings.

Lisa Farnsworth, at fifty, the oldest employee of the firm, had been Rigg's seamstress from the time he parted with his former partner. Before working for him, she'd worked for a time for Samuel Dyson for two years, and had worked for several other designers on a freelance basis.

The late Martha Frank, a few months younger than Farnsworth, had, like her, also worked for Dyson. The two women had worked together since their twenties.

Jason Lane, hired by Rigg after his previous assistant Stella Mason was killed by a hit-and-run driver, lived in Gaithersburg, Maryland. Prior to coming to work for Rigg, he'd been an accountant for an auto body shop in Gaithersburg, but had left suddenly. Heather couldn't find anything explaining his sudden departure, nor was there much else on him.

There wasn't, in fact, much on any of them – at least nothing to indicate that they wanted to do Rigg harm. On the contrary, he'd come through for most of them when others might have ignored them. Heather had truly dug up a ton of facts, but none of them moved us an inch closer to solving the mystery. She must have seen the disappointment on my face.

"Not much help, huh?" she asked.

"I don't know. We must be missing something here. I mean, none of this screams threats or extortion, and except for Kalishnakova, there's not much that anyone could use for blackmail."

Heather's pixie-like face took on a determined set. "Well, I guess that means I'll just have to dig deeper."

Heather's like a ferret when it comes to going after information. She's convinced that any case can be solved if only you can get enough of the right data. I, on the other hand, believe it's a matter of finding that one crucial piece of information and then finding a culprit's main vulnerability. We're polar opposites, but the truth is, it usually takes both of us working to our strengths and combining our talents to get to a solution. So, she would continue to mine the Internet and her contacts around town, while I would keep talking to people until someone sent a guilty signal my way.

"Okay, kid," I said. "You do that. I'll do a little digging of my own."

Just as she stood, the phone rang. She picked it up.

"A.E. Pennyback, Confidential Enquiries," she said. "How may I help you? Oh, sure, just a minute." She handed me the phone. "It's Calvin Rigg for you."

"Calvin, what can I do for you?"

"Al, I just got another call from that weird voice," he said. There was tension in his voice. "He . . . said that the price is now *two* million dollars, and I have 48 hours to pay or someone else will die. Thanks to Franklin's bequest I can probably scrape the money together, but it'll nearly bankrupt me."

The stakes in this little game of cat and mouse just got higher.

12.

With Rigg under a time constraint, Heather redoubled her efforts. I decided it was time to reach out for help. I made an appointment to have lunch with Buster Mayweather on Friday at our usual eatery, Mom's on Sixteenth Street.

Eating at Mom's was a kind of tradition Buster and I had established over more than a decade. It had begun around the time we first met, when he'd come to my house with two uniformed cops from Northern Virginia to inform me that my wife, Sara, and my son, Ethan, had been killed along with most of Ethan's soccer team when a truck driver had run a stop sign on Arlington Boulevard as the van Sara was driving was bringing them back from an evening junior league soccer match. Buster, a junior detective at the time, stayed with me through the identification procedure at the morgue, and for hours afterwards as I sat and stared at the walls of my living room. He'd been with me through making the funeral arrangements, and out of it all a kind of friendship had developed. His wife, Alma, and Sandra were best friends as well. Sandra and I were god parents to their twins, little Albert and Sandra. Even though Sandra and I aren't exactly the domestic type, we liked spending time with them in a family setting to watch the antics of the kids as they grew.

Mom's, though, was the equivalent of our man cave – it was where Buster and I went when we wanted some 'guy' time, or when one of us had a situation that he needed help from the other with.

Mom's was something of a Washington institution. Mom, who would never tell us her name, had come to Washington forty years earlier as a young woman from somewhere down south, and opened a soul food restaurant on Sixteenth Street in the District's Northwest section, not far from Howard University. The area had been one of the centers of black owned business until the rights of the 60s, especially the terrible violence that ensued after the assassination of Dr. Martin Luther King, Jr. in Memphis, when most of the buildings were either burned to the ground or trashed so badly they had to be condemned. Rumor has it that during all the violence, Mom's was never touched, and that, in fact, the rioters took their lunch breaks there.

The area started coming back in the late 1990s, with coffee shops, restaurants, and other business coming back to cater to Washington's upwardly mobile young population of all races. There in the middle of all this was Mom's, a few name changes and paint jobs later, still serving traditional southern food – heavy on the fat and mostly fried. Mom, too, had undergone change. Some of her older customers swear that as a younger woman she was slim, trim, and hot to trot. When Buster and I first started eating there, she was already over two hundred pounds of no-nonsense, southern black woman who wore print dresses that could have served as circus tents. She greeted each customer at the front door, pointed them to their favorite tables – for Buster and me it was the one in the right front corner with a view of the street and the entire interior of the place – and told them what the special of the day was. If you were one of her favorites – Buster and I fell into that category – she'd tell you what you were eating, and if you were smart, you didn't argue. Not only because she was now close to three hundred pounds, with biceps bigger around than my thighs, but because her husband was the cook, and the man was a master at his craft. His food melted in your mouth. And, Mom knew just what you wanted, sometimes even when you didn't.

Buster and I arrived at the same time, me coming in from south on Seventh Street and him on U Street from the west. He did an illegal U-turn and pulled in behind me, almost directly in front of Mom's. He put the 'Police Business' sign on his dash. I took the one he'd given me several months earlier and dropped it on the Bug's dash.

Mom was at her usual station, perched on a stool near the register on the order counter in front of the door, when we walked in. She was wearing a bright blue one-piece with a yellow and white checked apron around her ample waist. Her hair was pulled back severely and done in a bun in back.

"Well, if it ain't my favorite two boys," she said. "Y'all here for lunch." It wasn't a question.

"Sure thing, Mom," Buster said. "What you got good today?"

She scowled at him, raising a pudgy finger and stabbing the air in front of his face. "Everything I got is good, Buster Mayweather, and don't you go sayin' otherwise."

Mom is the only woman besides Alma who can cow Buster. He ducked his head into his massive shoulders and smiled shyly at her.

"'Course it is, Mom," he said. "Everybody knows that. That was just a figure of speech."

"Well, I figure you best be careful with your speech. Now, gone and sit down, while I gets your lunch ready. You boys want coffee?"

"I'd love a cup, Mom," I said.

She gently pinched my cheeks. "Now, here's a fella what knows how to be polite. You could learn a thing or two from him, Buster Mayweather," she said, frowning at Buster.

"I'd like a cup of coffee, too," Buster said.

"I know – with lots of cream and sugar," she said. "Now sit your butts down."

A stranger would think Mom didn't like Buster, but the fact is, she's like a mother to him – a stern mother, but a mother nonetheless. She gives him a hard time, but I feel sorry for anyone who goes after him in her presence. He adored her, too.

We took our usual table, me with my back against the wall, him to my right. I like being able to see outside and in, and prefer having something solid at my back. Buster humors me. He feels secure inside, but likes to keep an eye on his car and on the street outside.

Mom waddled over with our coffee, placing

the two oversized mugs precisely on the table near our right hands. Without a word, she went back to the kitchen.

"Okay, Al," Buster said. "What is it you want now?"

"Why does it have to be that I want something?" I held my hands up defensively. "Can't I just want to have lunch with my best friend?"

He made a snorting sound. "I ain't sayin' we ain't friends, dude, but I know you. When you call out of the blue and want to meet at Mom's, I know you workin' a case that got you in a corner, and you need something from me."

"I'm wounded to the core." I put a hand over my heart. "But, since you mention it, I do have a situation that I'd like to run past you. Sort of get your view as a police officer?"

"Okay, then," he said. "Long's we're straight with each other." He laughed. He actually liked getting involved in my cases – a change of pace from the gang slayings he usually had to deal with. "What is it you want to know?"

I gave him a rundown of the threats against Rigg, and a summary of what Heather had been able to dig up on everyone involved with him. While I was talking, Mom brought our food. Fried chicken, potato salad, collard greens, cornbread, and a pitcher of lemonade, with the promise of apple pie with ice cream for dessert. Buster wasted no time – while I talked the case, he dove in and began demolishing the food.

I alternated between telling my story and nibbling at the chicken and cornbread. By the time I'd finished the summary of my investigation, Buster was almost finished with his, and looking toward Mom for dessert. I'd managed to cut a big chunk out of the food piled on my own plate, and was wiping grease from my face and fingers.

"There you have it," I said. I took a sip of lemonade. It was a mixture of tart and sweet, just like I like it. "I have a pile of facts, but nothing that helps point me to who is making the threats or trying to extort money from Rigg."

"I see what you mean," he said. "This dude's got a bad luck cloud hanging over his head. Don't sound like it's a good idea to be working for him, 'specially if you happen to be a woman. First his assistant gets done in by a hit-and-run driver, and now one dies from a gas leak. Man!"

"Yeah, it's tough about Martha Frank. That puts him in a bind getting his dresses done up before his next big show. Speaking of the hit-and-run, though – that happened in the District. Did they ever find the driver who ran her over?"

"I don't know," he said. "I'll check it when I get back to the office. I doubt it, though. Hell, in the District, one in every six traffic fatalities is caused by a driver who fled the scene. We've got the highest rate of fatal hit-and-run accidents in the whole damn country."

"Holy crap," I said. "I know it's tough to be involved in that kind of accident, but I just don't see running away from it."

"Shit, man, depending on the circumstances, if you hit a pedestrian you can be charged with negligent homicide. That'll get you five years in the joint, and it's enough to cause most drivers to bolt. Most of the time, the driver is either drunk, or driving on an expired license or registration. We get 'em most of the time, but there are still a few unsolved cases, especially those that happen on back streets or after normal work hours."

Our conversation was interrupted by Mom, bearing a tray containing two humongous slices of fresh-baked apple pie with baseball-sized lumps of vanilla ice cream melting over the crust. The smell of cinnamon and baked apple made my mouth water. I quickly finished the rest of my main meal – Mom hates it when you leave food on the plate – and dug into the pie. I promised myself that I'd eat a light supper and run an extra mile on Saturday to work off the calories.

After coffee to wash everything down, Buster took off back to his place, and I went back to my office. I must have still smelled like fried chicken and apple pie – Heather wrinkled her nose and gave me a disapproving glance when I walked in. I left her muttering about fat and cholesterol and went into my office. After a lunch at Mom's all I felt like doing was taking a nap.

To keep from falling asleep, I took out my notebook and tried going over my notes, looking for something that I might have missed. I found nothing, and my eyelids kept drifting downward.

I was just about to give up fighting it when the phone rang. It was Buster.

"Hey, bro," he said. "I got a look at the Mason hit-and-run case. It's still unsolved."

He sounded wide awake. I've never understood how Buster does it. He can pack away enough food to fill three people, and it never seems to affect him.

"What can you tell me about it?" I asked, stifling a yawn.

I heard the rustling of papers. "The incident took place between 4:30 and 5:30 one morning, on Elm Street between Third and Fourth, near Howard University Hospital. Stella Mason lived in the area. According to the report, they think she was on her way to the Georgia Avenue bus stop in front of the hospital when she was struck as she was crossing Elm Street. Whoever hit her was either going pretty fast, or driving a pretty big vehicle. She was hit on the right side – broke both legs, her hip, most of her ribs, and her skull. ME said it looked like she banged into the vehicle before being tossed against the street about twenty feet from where she was initially hit. A neighbor of hers, who was on the way to the bus stop found her around 5:45, laying in the middle of the street. They pronounced her dead at the scene."

"There were no witnesses? No one saw or heard anything?"

"Naw," he said. "Not much traffic, vehicle or foot, in that neighborhood that time of morning, and they don't have traffic cameras. Whoever hit her got the hell out of there before the person who found the body came along. He didn't see anything."

"Do they have *any* idea who hit her? I mean, with all that damage to her body, the vehicle must have been damaged as well."

"Not much in the report, except they thought it might have been a commercial van or truck of some kind. They found bright yellow paint on her body and clothing on the right side. They put a dragnet out for commercial vehicles with yellow paint jobs, but nothing turned up."

"So, just another unsolved death in the nation's capital?"

"Another of the many we have," he said. "Oh, there was one other thing – there were no skid marks at the scene. Whoever hit her made no effort to stop, and didn't burn rubber leaving. Bastard probably saw what he'd done, saw there were no witnesses, and calmly drove away."

Charles Ray

13.

I got up early Saturday morning and kept my promise to myself to run an extra mile. Sandra decided to bag weekend exercise, and stayed in bed. I also put in an extra twenty minutes on the heavy bag, and, despite the chill in the February air, was sweating profusely when I left the barn and went back to the house to meditate and shower before waking Sandra for a light breakfast.

"Why do I have to starve myself at breakfast just because you pigged out at lunch yesterday?" she complained.

"Don't forget, we're having lunch with Blood and Elizabeth today, babe."

That caused her to snap her beautiful lips shut. Lucky me, too, because since moving in with me, she'd come to enjoy the weekend breakfasts when I pulled out all the stops in the kitchen. But, we both knew that a Saturday lunch with Carlton Raine meant a sumptuous southern style meal with all the trimmings, which one had to approach with a nearly empty stomach in order to fully appreciate and to avoid offending the host.

"Okay," she said. "But, I want extra toast."

So, she had a third slice of toast. I kept mine at one slice of toast, juice and coffee. I was planning to ask Raine a favor, so I definitely didn't want to offend him.

After finishing breakfast, we cleaned the kitchen – well, *I* cleaned it, while Sandra watched. Her punishment for the skimpy breakfast. Then, we just sat around listening to music on the radio until half past ten, when we hopped into my green Volkswagen for the drive to Raine's cabin.

The first day of February had been overcast, so according to legend, the groundhog didn't see his shadow, meaning winter would soon be over. While it was still a bit chilly, the snow had melted and the sky was powder blue and completely clear of clouds. It had been quite chilly during my morning run, but by midday the temperature had risen to a comfortable – sweat is enough – level. The trees were still bare, but the road to Raine's place was lined with evergreens, so I still couldn't spot the sensors and surveillance cameras I knew he had placed there to keep an eye on visitors.

The narrow, one lane track from River Road to his cabin curves a bit at first, but for the last quarter mile it's as straight as a ruler, giving him a good view of anyone on it. The cabin, which has nothing more than knee high within a hundred yards around it, is squat looking, with small opaque windows and slate roof. It looks a bit like a frontier fort at first glance, and that's in fact what it is. Raine has, in addition to his surveillance system, an arsenal sufficient to hold off a battalion, and the skills to use it.

As we came out of the last curve, I could see two columns of smoke ahead – one coming from the chimney, and a smaller one coming from a position just to the right of the structure. As I got closer I could see a figure standing near the corner, which soon resolved itself into Raine, wearing a knit cap and a light jacket, standing over a large metal grille from which the second column of smoke was coming.

He waved as I stopped the car. Sandra got out and walked over to give him a hug. I just waved back.

"What's up?" I asked.

"Just felt like having some grilled steak today," he said. "And, Elizabeth won't let me fire the grille up inside."

"That's because you can never get that awful smell out of upholstery and curtains," Elizabeth Sung said as she stepped off the cabin's front porch carrying a large platter of blood red meat cuts. She handed them to Raine, wiped her hands on the jeans that clung lovingly to her shapely legs, and gave Sandra a big hug and a kiss on the cheeks. She then walked over and gave me a brotherly peck on the cheek – no hug. "Would you guys like something to drink while the meat cooks?" She asked.

"I'd like a cold beer," Raine said. "And, I'll bet Al would too." He winked at me.

"Yes, I would," I said. Beer is not what I'd normally start with on a chilly day, but he wanted one, and we men have to stick together on these things.

Elizabeth frowned at the both of us, but turned and disappeared back inside the cabin. She emerged a few minutes later with two large bottles of *Qingdao* beer in her hands.

"I don't suppose it would do any good to ask the two of you to share one bottle, would it?" she asked.

"Aw, come on, hon," Raine said. "I don't want the lad to have to share my germs.

Besides, this is just enough to fortify me against the chill in the air."

Elizabeth is a lawyer, and a well-educated woman. She didn't buy that bull for a minute. But, she's also devoted to Raine – hell; they're devoted to each other, and have been since I introduced them – and so she allows him his little games. She made a face at him, but handed him the bottle anyway. She then handed me mine, giving me a slightly disapproving frown.

"Sandra, would you like to help me make potato salad?" she asked. "I suppose it's safe enough to leave these two juvenile delinquents alone out here."

Laughing, the two women went inside the cabin, arm in arm. I took a long pull from the bottle. Chilly it might be, but the slightly acrid stuff felt good sliding down my throat. That first beer *always* tastes good. Raine lifted his bottle in a toast.

"Here's to a beverage that's as old as wine," he said, referring to something I hadn't known until he told me that evidence had been found that the Egyptians and Romans had brewed beer, meaning that beer and wine predated whiskey by a long stretch of time. "And, to the beautiful women who serve it."

"I'll drink to that." I lifted my bottle, and took another swallow.

He put his bottle on the wooden tray attached to the side of the grille, and began placing the inch-thick steaks over the simmering pieces of wood. As the meat began to sizzle, the smell of roasting flesh mixed with the sweet aroma of hickory, activating my salivary glands. Raine saw the effect and grinned.

"Doesn't have to be summer for a barbecue, eh?" I could only nod. "How did that ID work for you?" he asked, deftly changing the subject.

"Worked like a charm," I said. I described how I'd figured out the insurance scam, and the fee I would be getting for it. "Now, I can concentrate on Calvin Rigg's situation."

"That's your fashion designer friend, right? You mentioned something last time about him being threatened."

Between sips of beer I filled him in on the case. He just nodded occasionally. Raine is a good listener. He had to be to succeed as one of the first black field agents for the Central Intelligence Agency, hired before affirmative action was the law of the land. He'd learned to listen to, evaluate, and file away massive amounts of information, and act on it when necessary.

"Sounds like Mr. Rigg has himself a whale of a problem," he said when I'd finished.

"And, sounds like you're up a tree trying to solve it."

"Or up a creek without a paddle," I said. I laughed at his wince. Okay, it wasn't the most original statement, but clichés become clichés because they're true.

"Your problem, Al, is that you're over thinking this whole thing."

"Over thinking – in what way am I *over* thinking? I have all this information, none of which tells me a damn thing."

"Well, for a start, you're looking far afield for your perpetrator," he said. "And, you're looking for a complex motive."

"Hell, someone's jacking Rigg up for two million bucks. You don't call that complex?"

"No, Al. I call that expensive. Look, let's review what you know, okay?"

That didn't take too long. I knew that someone was demanding two million dollars from Calvin Rigg. I knew that some of his models had been threatened. I told him that.

"That," he said. "Is *not* all that you know about this situation."

"Okay, you tell me – what else do I know about it?"

He picked up his bottle and took a sip.

After putting it down, he turned and faced me. "Well, have you thought about the *real* motive behind all this? Rigg is being extorted for a goodly sum of money. At the same time, his models are being pressured to quit. Why?"

"I figure it's aimed to drive him out of business," I said. It seemed simple to me.

"Why do both? Wouldn't having to fork over that much money drive him into bankruptcy?"

"Well, yes, I suppose it would."

"And, there's no guarantee that the models quitting would really disrupt his business all that much, right?"

"Right. In fact, the seamstresses and the makeup guy are the real keys. I mean, losing one seamstress has already put pressure on him for his upcoming show. I'm told that the models quitting would only be a momentary hiccup."

"So, son," he said. "Ask yourself – why would someone hit him with both barrels like that?" He looked at me like a teacher prompting a slow student. "Aw, come on, Al. It *has* to be about more than just driving him out of business."

When he said it like that, it made sense – sort of. There was just one hitch.

"Okay, I'll buy it. It has to be about more than running him out of business. Problem is – what *is* it about?"

He laughed. "I can't answer all your questions, son. You have to do some work yourself. I will leave you with this, though. Remember the theory of Occam's Razor."

"Oca what?" I asked. Raine had a somewhat annoying habit of bringing up things that were way outside my usual frame of reference.

"Occam's Razor," he said, laughing. "It's a theory that was developed by William of Occam, a 14th century Franciscan friar. Basically, he said that when a problem has two competing solutions, the simpler one is usually the correct one."

"Okay, I see your point," I said. "Now, as soon as I have two solutions to Rigg's problem, I'll know which one to choose. Of course, right now, I don't have even one."

He looked down at the steaks. They were now a golden brown with black streaks. He poked one with a knife, twisting the blade to show the pink interior.

"Nothing activates the brain cells like a good dose of protein," he said. "And, these steaks look ready. Why don't we take them inside and marry them up with Elizabeth's potato salad. She made garlic bread too."

Rigg's and Occam's razor would just have to wait. I had an appointment with a thick, medium rare piece of beef.

14.

On Monday, after checking in with Heather at the office, and learning, in order, that she'd spent the weekend cleaning out her closets and hadn't found any new information to help with Rigg's case, I drove to Georgetown and Rigg's studio.

The place was a madhouse. The reception area had pressed into service as a rehearsal hall of sorts, and Calvin Rigg stood in the center near the desk, shouting orders to the models who scurried back and forth; Lisa Farnsworth, who alternated between making alterations on dresses and helping the models slip into and out of them; and Greg Cheney who stood off to the side with a sketch pad on which he was daubing colors on sketchily drawn faces.

Tillie the receptionist had been pressed

into service as Farnsworth's assistant. She was running to and fro, moving rolls and folds of fabric at the seamstress's direction. Caleb Billings stood in the corner, leaning on a broom handle – occasionally walking over and sweeping cuttings from around Farnsworth.

At first, no one noticed me when I stepped out of the elevator.

Just as he was bending to adjust Bib's hemline, Rigg noticed me. He let the cloth flap against her shapely brown calf, stood, and rushed over.

"Tell me you've learned something," he said. "Please tell me this nightmare is over."

The fingers of his hands wrestled with each other as he looked at me plaintively. His brow was shiny with sweat, and his lower lip quivered.

"I wish I could say it is, but I'm close – I'm pretty sure of that. How are you holding up?"

"Okay so far," he said. "It's been tough with Martha gone, though. Lisa's a champ, and I still remember how to cut, but I have so many other things to do, I'm not much help to her."

"Any more threats or calls?"

"I didn't get any," he said. He looked up at

Bibi Gunn. "Any of you girls get called this weekend?"

She shook her head. "I didn't," she said. "And, since I haven't heard anyone bitching about calls this morning, I think you can assume that no one else did either."

His expectant gaze returned to me. "Do you think this means he's given up?"

I shook my head.

"Not likely," I said. "I think he was just taking a break."

His eyes glistened. "Damn, this shit's starting to get to me. I don't know how much more I can take."

He seemed on the verge of a meltdown, but who could blame him? His models threatened because of him. A demand that he turn over all his money, leaving himself flat busted. Most people would have imploded long before. But for the fact that he'd gone through hell when he'd been accused of murdering his partner, he might have.

Then, a thought came to me. As I watched the play of tortured emotions on Rigg's face, I realized that the motive for all this was probably not driving him out of business – it might be to drive him crazy. Having to bear the blame for anything happening to his models, the feeling of loss over the death of

Martha Frank – coming close on the heels of the death of his previous assistant, Stella Mason – would be putting him under intense pressure, pressure that if not relieved could drive him over the edge. It made sense. More sense than sheer greed or desire to get rid of a competitor. Now, all I had to do was determine who had it in for him enough to want to do him that much harm.

"Hang in there, partner," I said. "I haven't given up yet."

The phone on the reception desk rang. All movement stopped. Everyone stared at the jangling instrument. Finally Tillie Moyer dashed over and answered.

"Rigg's Rigs," she said brightly. "How may I direct your call?"

Her face contorted, and she held the instrument away from her head.

"What is it, Tillie?" Rigg asked.

"It's t-that voice," she said. "Wants to s-speak to you."

He looked wide-eyed at me.

"When you get him on," I said just above a whisper. "Try to keep him talking and hand the phone to me."

His head bobbed up and down. He had a

dazed expression on his face. Tillie held the phone out to him. He took it holding it as it was a poisonous snake.

He took a deep breath. "H-hello," he said.

Then, he shoved the phone at me.

"-have eleven days to get me the money," a metallically distorted voice said in my ear. "Fail to pay up and someone else will die."

"Who the hell is this?" I asked.

After a long pause the voice continued. "Mr. Pennyback. You think you can help him. You can't. No one can help him. He must pay."

Then the connection was broken, leaving only the humming sound of the phone in my ear.

"W-what did he say?" Rigg asked.

"Probably the same as before," I said. "Pay up or else."

"You have any idea who it is?"

"No. As I suspected, he's using some kind of voice distortion device. If I had a recording, I have a friend who could probably clean it up enough to get a recognizable sound. You don't happen to have recording on this phone system, do you?"

"Unfortunately, I don't," he said. "So, where does that leave us?"

"With a lot of work to do to find out who it is." I placed the phone back on the cradle. "But, I will find out. You can count on that."

I wished I felt as confident as I sounded. It was important, though, to keep him bucked up. From the expression on his face, he was pretty close to crumbling. I considered suggesting he buy a recorder, but that would have been closing the barn door after the horses have been stolen, and wouldn't be done in time to do us much good.

"What will you do now?" he asked.

"My partner's working on some leads," I lied. A necessary lie, though, to try and keep his spirits up. "I'll go back to the office and see what I can do to run them down."

With a crestfallen look and slumped shoulders, he turned away. I turned to go. Lisa Farnsworth walked over and stood in front of me.

"Mr. Pennyback, I'd like to talk to you in private if you don't mind."

She put a hand on my arm and walked me over near the elevator.

"What do you want to talk about?" I asked.

"I've been thinking about Martha," she said in a quiet voice. "The more I think about what happened, the more it bothers me."

I put a hand on her shoulder. "I know it must be hard for you – losing a close friend like that. But, these things happen. She just had a bit too much to drink and fell asleep with a gas heater going. It happens too often in cold weather."

She shook her head and glared at me. "Not to Martha," she said. "I've known – I knew her since we were just young girls getting started in this business. Yeah, we'd take a drink now and then; even tie one on for special occasions. The three of us, Martha, Stella, and me, we'd sometimes go out after work and close the Georgetown bars. But, we had one iron-clad rule – we always kept one sober person in the group. We never drank too much when we were with strangers, or when we were alone. That's the way you get in trouble."

"But, she was at home," I said. "She probably felt safe there. Besides, you guys have been under a lot of pressure lately."

"I'm telling you, she'd never sit home alone and get that drunk. She'd only do that if she was with someone she knew and trusted."

I was getting an uneasy feeling. "Are you

saying that you don't think her death was an accident?"

She blinked and looked at me as if she was just seeing me.

"Yeah, I think that's what I'm saying."

15.

Processing Lisa Farnsworth's bombshell was interrupted by the sound of agitated talking in the middle of the room. I turned to see Calvin Rigg sitting on the floor, his legs splayed out in front and his head in his hands.

"I can't do it. I'm sorry," he was saying. "I don't want anyone else hurt."

Everyone was crowding around him. Greg Cheney leaned over and massaged his shoulder.

"Hey, Cal," he said. "I know how you feel, but you can't give up now."

There were nods and murmurs of agreement.

"That's right," Genvieve Montand said,

running a hand through her close-cropped brown hair. "If you quit now, the bad guys will have won."

Rigg shook his head. He looked up at them, tears spilling from his bloodshot eyes.

"What chance do we have?" he said. "We're behind schedule. I don't think we'll have all the dresses done up in time. And, I don't want to be responsible for anyone else being hurt."

"If you quit," Bibi Gunn said, her hands on her hips. "It means we'll be out of work. If you don't think that hurts, you ain't never been out of work. You think about that?"

Farnsworth pushed past me and walked over, squatting in front of Rigg. "Now, you listen to me, Calvin Rigg," she said. "You are *not* quitting on us now. This show is your ticket to fame, and if you become famous, we benefit. You quit, and there's no one in this town who'd give us the time of day."

"I know all that, Lisa," he said. "But, Martha's dead, and you guys are being threatened. Besides, I don't think we can get all the dresses done in time."

"Oh, pish," she said. "We can do it. Even if we have to work a little overtime."

"Besides, even if you don't get *all* the dresses done, what does it matter?" Greg

Cheney said. "The audience isn't gonna know which dresses aren't shown. They'll only care about the ones they see."

Rigg looked from one to the other. Then, his head swiveled around to take in the rest of the room. Everyone looked at him expectantly – even Moyer and Billings. He was wavering. I was being paid to find out who was threatening him, not be a counselor or baby sitter, but his people were right, if he quit now, he would be a loser.

"Look, Calvin," I said. "They're right, you know. You can't quit just because things are a little dark. If they're willing to back you, you have no reason to quit. Trust me – I'll find this guy."

He wiped the tears from his cheeks. Then, he levered himself to a standing position and took a deep breath. He covered his face for a few minutes, breathing deeply. I worried that he might hyperventilate, but he finally stopped and dropped his hands and smiled wanly.

"You guys are the greatest," he said. "I don't know what to say."

"Just say the show's on," Farnsworth said.

His smile widened.

"The show's on," he said. "The fucking

show is *on!* Now, let's get to work."

I left them as they got back to work.

As I was paying the parking fee at the entrance to the garage, I noticed a flash of yellow out of the corner of my eye. It was Jason Lane in his jeep, pulling into the garage. He was staring straight ahead, frowning, and didn't seem to notice me.

16.

With things back to what passes for normal at Rigg's studio, I went back to the office where Heather glumly informed me she'd found nothing new. In the meantime, I sat at my desk trying to process what Lisa Farnsworth had told me.

The next day, I called Buster, who called in a favor with a Montgomery County Police detective he knew, and got the information on Martha Frank's death.

When the police arrived, the smell of gas was powerful. They broke down the door and found her sitting in a chair in her living room, an empty vodka bottle on the floor near her chair and an empty glass next to her right foot. She was pronounced dead at the scene. The body was taken to the morgue in Rockville where an autopsy was performed to determine cause of death, but the detective at the scene wrote in the report that there were no signs of foul play, assault or forced entry, and the likelihood was the victim had died from the gas leak.

The autopsy confirmed that assumption. Martha Frank, a fifty-three-year-old white female, weighed 140 pounds at the time of her death. She was in relatively good health for her age. The tox screen of her blood showed a blood alcohol level of 0.28, which was way over the legal limit and sufficient to cause unconsciousness in a woman her size. Moreover, the lab had found traces of methane, ethane, propane, butane, and the other components found in natural gas. The coroner had ruled that, based on the physical evidence found at the scene, and the absence of any evidence showing that anyone else had been present in the room where the victim was found, death was due to asphyxiation caused by carbon monoxide poisoning – no foul play.

Those were the facts. Just another unfortunate accidental death, not unheard of during the winter. But, Lisa Farnsworth was convinced that her friend had not died accidentally. When she told me that, she hadn't sounded crazy or delusional or like she was making it up – it had been, as far as I could tell from her facial expressions and body language, the plain, simple truth. It wasn't exactly a *fact*, but it had the ring of truth.

But, that meant that someone had killed Frank. Someone had somehow introduced an almost lethal amount of alcohol into her system, and then left her to breathe in gas until her lungs and heart stopped functioning. That had the ring of cold-blooded, calculated murder. It *had* somehow to be connected to the actions against Rigg. How and by whom were the big questions that I had to answer, and the clock was ticking. First, I had to review all the facts we'd gathered so far. Then, I needed to discard those not pointing to the simplest solution – the ones that didn't seem to fit the *truth*.

I'd reached that inevitable point in my investigation when frustration threatens to set in; when I've run into a brick wall that was too high to climb, set too deep in the earth to tunnel underneath, and that stretched too far to each side to map out a way around. At times like this, most people go blank and think of giving up. Or, they let anger send their thoughts into a tailspin, ideas spinning around in utter confusion, chasing up one blind alley after another. My brain, though, doesn't work that way. I'm addicted to puzzles. I don't believe in unsolvable puzzles. I get calm. I meditate. I don't force it. Instead, I let the facts spin as they will, and wait until I see the ones that seem to fit. When I do, I don't try to force them into place. I let them continue to spin until they drop in place of their own accord.

I knew that I had most of the pieces needed for a solution. There was just that *one* piece missing. The piece, that when it appeared, would make sense of everything else.

There would, I knew, be more odd bits and pieces of information floating into view. Some would be useful, but most would be meaningless. But, if I got myself centered – in harmony with my surroundings – I'd be able to recognize the important pieces.

As often happens when I'm at that point, a part of my mind drifted back in time. The old Korean man who taught me martial arts also taught me to meditate properly. His advice was, when you're on the verge of frustration let your mind find a happy place. My happy place was the time I'd had with Sara and Ethan before a truck driver in a hurry had taken them away from me. Not that being with Sandra didn't make me happy, mind you. She did. Just not in the same way I'd been happy with my late wife and son. Sandra and I didn't talk about that, but I knew that she knew. She understood. Which is why I'd come to love her.

I sat back in my chair, relaxing my body one muscle group at a time, breathing in and out in an even rhythm, feeling the air as it passed into and out of my nostrils. I could feel the steady beating of my heart – the warm flow of blood through my veins and arteries. Without consciously listening, I could hear the dull thrum of traffic on Fourth Street, the whisper of wind blowing through the bare trees outside my window, the steady hum of the heating system. I could even hear the faint clicking sound of Heather's fingers stabbing at her keyboard outside.

When I've reached my center, I am totally relaxed. Not sleepy, or in a trance. On the contrary, I am wide awake and aware of everything around me. But, I'm also able to tap into my dreams. I can see everything in my field of vision, but I can also *see* what's in my mind – most importantly, I can see my happy place.

I see my son, Ethan, playing in the tiny backyard of the house we'd rented in the District of Columbia when I'd been transferred from Fort Bragg to the Pentagon. I see Sara, her small shapely body covered by a one-piece dress, but clearly visible through the thin fabric – aware that I'm ogling her, and enjoying it. She was comfortable in her own sexuality, never flaunting it, but nor did she hide it. She'd been that way from the first. I met her when I was on temporary duty in the Philippines to help the army there fight the separatist guerillas in the south. Her father was the general in charge of the unit I was assigned to train. He'd invited me to his house for supper to welcome me. Sara, his oldest daughter, had assumed the role of hostess after her mother died, and I'd been smitten at the first sight of her. I could tell she liked me too. It took a bit longer to convince her father that we were right for each other. Even though he consented to the marriage, he was cold to me until Ethan was born. The sight of his first grandson, though, melted the old man's heart. The sight of my first and only son had melted my heart as well. I'd never been all that good around kids until Ethan. Like his mother, he had a way of worming his way inside you – burrowing deep down where you live.

I was well into my happy place. Unlike my dreams, I couldn't communicate with Sara and Ethan when I meditated. I just enjoyed *seeing* them. In the background, my mind was working on the case. Looking at every piece of evidence we'd acquired, assessing every individual, looking for connections.

I could feel the start of something when the buzz of the phone yanked me out of my meditative state.

I snatched up the receiver. "Yeah? What is it?" I said. I knew it had to be important. Heather knew that I was meditating, and while she didn't see the value of it herself, she knew how useful it was to me, and never interrupted me while I was doing it unless it was necessary.

"Greg Cheney on the line for you, boss," she said simply. "He sounds frantic."

I had her put him through.

"Greg, what's up?" I asked.

"Some fuck tried to run me over this morning," he said. There was a mixture of panic and anger in his voice. "Imeantriedtorunmeoffthefuckingroad!"

"Who, man," I said. "Slow down, take a deep breath and run – no walk – that by me again."

I could hear his ragged breathing over the line.

"Last night I went up to Mount Airy to a party with some friends of mine," he said. "I was on my way back around 3:30 this morning, just south of Damascus on Ridge Road, when a car came out of a ride road and tried to ram me. I just saw it out of the corner of my eye and jammed on the gas. That's all kept the bastard from smashing into the driver's side door. He clipped my rear bumper, though. Nearly caused me to go off the road."

"Did you get a look at the car or driver?" I asked.

"No, man - it was dark that time of morning. All I saw was these two headlights coming at me. When the fucker clipped me, I went into a skid. I was pretty occupied keeping my car on the road. I finally got it straightened out and I jammed it to the floor to get the hell out of there."

"What happened after that?"

"I think he might have chased me a ways, but I pretty soon came to Damascus, and he dropped back."

"You sure this wasn't just an accident – some drunk driver who wasn't watching where he was going?" A small part of my mind was saying that given the circumstances this was unlikely, but I wanted to hear what he thought about it.

"I don't think so," he said. "I mean, one minute it's dark, and the next these headlights flash on and this dude's trying to run me over. That sound like an accident to you?"

Under any other circumstances, I might have argued with him. The eyes can play tricks on you at night, and he'd probably been drinking, which would have affected his ability to see and remember clearly. But, given all that had happened, it would have to be a coincidence that another key player in Rigg's fashion studio would be the victim of an *accident* – especially following so closely on the heels of the previous accident. I'm aware that coincidences can happen – I just don't happen to believe in them.

"No, that doesn't sound like an accident. I just wish you'd seen something that might help us identify this person."

"Sorry, man," he said. "I was kinda busy trying not to get killed. Next time I'll try to be more observant."

The note of sarcasm was good. It meant he'd gotten past the fear of what had almost happened. You should never let your anger get out of control and rule your behavior, but a little anger can be a cleansing emotion.

"Don't worry about it. I'm just glad you're not hurt. Did you report it to the police?"

"Yeah, I stopped in Damascus and reported it. They sent a car out to where it happened, but didn't find anything. They also checked my car. There was a black smudge on the left rear, and they're checking it out, but the cop said it looked like common black paint you might find on any one of thousands of cars. Not much help in tracking down the guy that hit me."

"Let me know if they find anything, okay?"

He promised he would. I broke the connection. More facts to process. There was something, but it was vague – some fact that tied everything together. If only I could separate it from the mass of information we had.

17.

My meditative state had been disrupted. I was giving serious consideration to bagging it and going home for the day. Heather walked in with a noncommittal look on her cherubic face and a notebook in her hand.

"What's up honey bunch?" I asked.

"I was running some more background checks on everyone at Calvin's studio, and I came up with a few anomalies on Jason Lane," she said.

"Rigg's assistant? What kind of anomalies?"

"There are all these gaps in his record. I have him going to Montgomery College after high school and getting an associate degree in accounting, and then going to work as a book keeper for an auto body shop in

Gaithersburg. Then, he quits that job for no apparent reason, and reappears as Calvin Rigg's assistant."

"I'm not following you, kid," I said. "We already knew all that."

"I know, I know," she said, pouting. "But, could you please let me do this my way. It's the only way I can make sense of things. Unlike you, I can't jump into a problem in the middle and understand it."

Heather's mind works like a computer. It starts at the beginning, and works methodically through to the end. She doesn't handle diversions well. Me, on the other hand, I think I'm all about diversions. But, if I wanted to know what she knew, I had to let her do it her way.

"Okay, I'm sorry. Go on with your story."

'Thank you." She snapped open her notebook. "That was just to set the stage for the rest. Jason Lane's mother was named Caroline Lane. His father, George, died when he was six. Caroline raised him alone until she died during his sophomore year in high school."

"And, that's an anomaly?"

"No, but the fact that I can't find a record of him being put into foster care is," she said. "He was sixteen when his mother died, a minor, so social services should have put him into some kind of foster care, and there should be a record of it. I can't find a record. All I can find is a brief mention of him living with a woman named Albertina Lane the year he graduated from high school. I got that from the school records. After that, because he was eighteen, he was considered an adult. He moved out on his own."

"Did you find out who Albertina Lane is?" I asked.

"No, I'm still checking that. I assume it was maybe an aunt on his father's side, but other than the mention in the school records, I can't find the name anywhere."

Like I've already said, my mind doesn't work like the ordinary person's. I process information organically. I can see connections that linear thinkers miss. Something clicked in my mind – Albertina – there was a connection there.

"While you're checking," I said. "Run a deep background check on Albertina Wittmer."

"That's the woman who killed Rigg's former partner isn't it? I thought her name was Tina."

"Her first name was Albertina, but everyone called her Tina."

"You think Albertina Lane and Albertina Wittmer are the same person?"

"That's not exactly your everyday name, you'll have to admit," I said. "If she is, it puts a whole new light on this case."

"She was sentenced to twenty to life for killing Franklin Honeywell. She's in Lorton. How could she be involved in this?"

"I don't know, but I plan to ask her," I said. "Now start digging into her background. See if there's a connection between her and Jason Lane."

"Considering that you helped put her in Lorton, are you sure she'll even talk to you?"

I hadn't really thought it out that far. Getting in to see a prisoner in Lorton was a bit more difficult than visiting one in the DC Corrections Facility, where I could use Buster's connections. It was time to reach out to Quincy.

I dialed his number, and waited while his secretary pulled him from a meeting.

His reaction, when I told him what I wanted, was shock.

"Why the devil do you want to visit a woman you helped put in prison?" he asked.

I explained my theory about the threats

against Calvin Rigg.

"I just have a few questions for her," I said.

There was a long pause. I heard the rustling of papers.

"Okay," he said finally. "It'll take a few days. I have to get you on her authorized visitors' list, and that'll take her okay. I can maybe get her lawyer to talk her into doing it. I'm guessing you want to do this right away."

"Tomorrow if possible," I said.

"Ain't gonna happen, amigo," he said. "I'll push it as hard as I can, but don't expect anything for at least two or three days."

There was no point harassing him any more than I had to. I knew he'd move things as fast as possible. If I had to wait three days, I'd wait. That would be faster than I could do it on my own. I thanked him and rang off.

18.

If you ever decide to visit an inmate in prison, think long and hard about it. If it's not a close relative, or there's not a strong professional reason, you might want to consider writing a letter instead, and even letters are screened – incoming and outgoing.

First, Quincy had to convince Tina Wittmer's lawyer to convince her to add me to her list of authorized visitors. That took a day. I think she was curious about why I wanted to see her. Or, maybe she still had a bit of a thing for me. She'd come on to me when we first met. I then had to submit a request to visit. Quincy pulled some strings at the Justice Department, and they put pressure on the DC authorities to allow me to make my request by phone rather than mail, which would have added a week or more to the process. The clerk who took my call got back to me the next day, approving my request to visit for that Wednesday, as Quincy had predicted, three days after we started the process.

I'd also been lucky, Quincy informed me, in the timing of my request. Action was underway to close Lorton prison, he said, with most of its inmates being transferred to a private-run facility somewhere in North Carolina. Not only would that have been a longer drive, but I could imagine the bureaucratic red tape was even more snarled. I don't much like dealing with the government bureaucracy. The thought of dealing with a civilian bureaucracy performing what should be a government function made my scalp itch. I had a special dislike for the concept of privately run prisons – a symbol of our cultural preference for incarceration over rehabilitation.

The day for my visit dawned bright, cold, and clear. I'd been given a 2:00 p.m. visit time. I figured the driving time from my office, south on I-95 to Lorton, at about an hour, so I ate an early lunch and left DC at 12:00 to give myself time for the prison entry procedures. I hadn't figured on the government workers who leave their offices early on Friday to get a jump on the weekend. It took me 90 minutes to get to the Lorton off ramp, and I almost got side swiped by some fool in a BMW who changed lanes in front of me without signaling, so that he could get around the car in front of him that had only been going fifteen over the speed limit – which was too slow for him. If there's a stretch of road in the Washington metro area that I hate more than the Beltway, it's I-95. The main north-south interstate, connecting New England with Florida, attracts some of the world's worst, most inconsiderate drivers.

Thankfully, once off I-95, the traffic was light. Furnace Road to Lorton Road to Ox Road, and a short stretch to 9601 Ox Road and the sign indicating visitor parking. Except for my ID, notebook, and a pen, I took everything else out of my pockets. An unsmiling guard at the entrance, after checking to ensure my name was on his list, still patted me down after running his detection wand over me from head to foot. I was directed through a series of locked doors, each closed securely before the next could be opened, to a small windowless room containing a plain metal table bolted to the floor, and two chairs opposite each other at the table. The walls were bare except for the placard containing the rules for visitors – only brief hugs and handshakes allowed; no transfer of packages, papers or objects; no food or drink; no smoking. Another unsmiling guard opened the door to let me in, and then positioned himself outside the door.

I'd been sitting there for ten minutes when

a guard brought Tina Wittmer in.

I almost didn't recognize her. Her brown hair had been cut short, almost a crew cut, causing her ears to stick out from her head. She'd put on a few pounds, but it looked like muscle rather than fat. The pixie-like look that I remembered had been replaced by a hard wariness. She was dressed in a blue jump suit with no pockets. A number was stenciled over the left breast. She wore plain leather shoes without laces. Her hands were cuffed at her waist.

The guard led her to the chair opposite me and nudged her down.

"Are the cuffs really necessary?" I asked.

He gave me a hard look, and then shrugged. "Suit yourself," he said, removing the cuffs. "You have thirty minutes."

I waited until he'd gone. "Thanks for seeing me, Tina," I said.

She looked at me, her eyelids half lowered. Her expression was unreadable.

Finally, she leaned forward, her small breasts pressing against the edge of the table. Her lips turned up in a half-smile.

"Why do you want to talk to me?" she asked.

The signs of flirtation that I'd seen when we first met were gone. She eyed me like a cat watching a bird with a broken wing – like she was trying to decide when to pounce.

"I'm working for Calvin Rigg," I said. "And, something's come up that I'd like to ask you about."

She laughed - mirthless, harsh sound coming from deep in her throat.

"What could I possibly tell you? I've been cooped up in this hell hole since the trial." She leaned farther forward. "How's old Cal doing these days? I imagine he's made a comeback since he got cleared."

"Yeah," I said. "His designs are catching on. There's a rumor that some big outfit in New York is interested."

Her face turned cold, and her lips curled downward.

"Interested in *his* designs? I'll just bet. I understand he inherited Franklin's estate – is that true?"

"As a matter of fact, it is."

"That means he got all of the designs that Franklin never got a chance to show."

"I suppose so," I said. I was losing control of the conversation. "But, that doesn't have anything to do with why I wanted to talk to you."

"Maybe," she said. "But, it's why I agreed to talk to you. I'll bet the designs that are catching on came from Franklin's stash."

I shrugged. "I have no idea, but what does that have to do with anything?"

"That bastard was showing my work, and taking all the credit for it." She closed her eyes. Her cheeks, pale from lack of sunshine, showed two spots of pink. "That's why I killed him, you know."

That and the fact that her brain cells had been scrambled by all the cocaine she sucked up her nose – but, I didn't mention that. I needed to get her back to why I really came.

"Okay, but could we get back to why I really came? What does Franklin using your designs have to do with what's happening now?"

"You're the hotshot detective," she said. "You figure it out. Now, what was it you wanted to ask me?"

"Does the name Caroline Lane mean anything to you?"

"No, why should it?" she answered quickly. Too quickly.

"How about Jason Lane?"

Her eyes flickered. "Never heard of him," she said. "Why are you asking me these questions?"

Again, she answered too quickly. A sure sign she was lying.

"What is your mother's name?" I asked.

She opened her mouth, and then closed it, glaring at me. "Why the hell do you want to know?"

"Let's just say I'm trying to make sense of some information that has come into my possession. It's a simple question – what's your mother's name?"

"Well, here's a simple answer – it's none of your fucking business. Next question."

She clamped her lips shut, and sat there glaring at me. She leaned back in the chair.

"Is Jason Lane your brother?" I asked.

"Fuck you," she said.

"Are you working with Jason Lane to extort money from Calvin Rigg?"

She folded her arms across her breasts and smiled at me. "Now, why would I want to do a thing like that? It's not like I have a lot of things to spend money on in here for the next twenty years."

Look for the simple solution, I thought. Then, it hit me. If Calvin Rigg was using the designs he'd inherited from Franklin Honeywell, he was using her designs. He might not even know that he was. But, she would. She'd killed her former boss for doing the very same thing.

"Maybe, it's not about the money," I said. "Maybe you just want him to suffer."

She gave a look that would frost a window.

"Guard," she yelled. "Take me back to my cell. This visit is over. Don't bother asking to come back. You're off my authorized visitor's list."

19.

It was a bit after four when I got back to the office.

"Did you get anything useful from Tina Wittmer?" Heather asked when I walked in.

"I did," I said. "She's Jason Lane's older sister. She didn't admit to it, but when I mentioned him and his mother, I saw a flicker of recognition in her eyes. I wonder if we could find out if he's on her visitor's list."

"I could try, but I doubt it. It would be a violation of the privacy act for them to release that information to anyone but the police."

I could get Buster to ask for it, but since I was pretty sure Tina and Jason were related, it didn't seem necessary. Besides, even Buster can only make the bureaucracy move so fast, and time was running out. I needed to do something quickly to bust the case.

"Doesn't matter, I suppose," I said. "I guess I'll just have to work on Lane himself. Have you picked up anything else on him?"

"Yeah, I located the place where he used to work." She flipped through her notebook. "Here it is – a place called Bubba's Body Works, on Park Avenue in Old Town Gaithersburg."

"Maybe I'll drop in on them on Monday and see what they can tell me. In the meantime, I'm going home. I owe Sandra an evening out."

20.

On Monday, I called Heather and let her know that I was going to Gaithersburg before coming to the office.

I left home around 8:30, taking a left off River Road onto Travilah Road, a two-lane route lined on both sides by trees, behind which sit an assortment of dwellings ranging from mini-mansions to old farm houses until you get to the intersection with Dufief Mill Road, which is an even narrower street that runs north to Maryland Route 28, where it becomes Muddy Branch Road, a wider road that ends at West Diamond Avenue, where I turned right and drove into Gaithersburg's old town, hear the railroad station. I took a left onto North Summit, which transits the historic section of town, and after a block,

turned left onto Brookes Avenue. The first
cross street was Park Avenue, and Bubba's
Body Works was a squat concrete showroom
attached to a large metal hangar-like building
at the corner. The parking area was a part-
gravel, part-dirt cleared area to the side of
the metal building, containing a number of
cars with various degrees of rust coating the
exteriors, one or two late model cars that sat
low to the ground, and six or seven pickup
trucks. Three of the pickups had rebel flag
decals on the bumpers. When I got out of my
Volkswagen, which looked out of place among
so many big, mostly American, cars, I could
hear the muffled sound of metal on metal
from the metal building.

I headed for the concrete building, the
front of which was mostly glass through
which I could see shelf upon shelf of auto
parts and accessories. A bell over the door
tinkled as I entered. A buxom brunette
wearing powder blue coveralls open at the
throat to more effectively display her wares
looked up smiling as I approached the
counter that ran almost all the way across
the back of the place.

"High, what can we do for you this
morning?" she asked brightly.

I showed her my ID. "I'm looking for
Bubba," I said.

She gave me a funny look. Then, she shook her head, causing a lock of hair to flop over her eyes. She tossed it daintily away.

"There's no one here named Bubba," she said.

"This is Bubba's Body Works, right?"

She looked confused. She shook her head again, like a dog shaking off water. Then, she laughed.

"Oh, yeah, the name," she said. "I guess I can see how that might confuse you. You looking for the owner of the place?"

"Yes."

"His name's Daryl Jackson, not Bubba."

She looked as if she expected me to ask why a man named Daryl would call his business Bubba's Body Works. I disappointed her. I didn't give a damn.

"Is he around?" I asked.

She looked disappointed.

"Yeah," she said, sticking her lips out in a little pout. "You want to talk to him?"

"That would be nice."

"He's over in the body shop," she said. She pointed to a green door to her right. "You can go through there, or you can go back outside and go through the front. It's shorter through the door over there."

"Thank you," I said.

The metal building looked larger on the inside than it had looked from the outside. To the right of the door was a partitioned area with a large window. Inside the area I could see a tall, broad shouldered man with unruly brown hair and several days' growth of beard, waving his finger in the face of a smaller man with lank blond hair mostly covered by a John Deere cap.

It was noisy, but not much more than it had been from outside. A number of mechanics were working on vehicles around the large open area, some over pits, some up on hoists. Several of the cars were painted in racing colors.

I assumed the big guy was Daryl Jackson. I walked over to the partition and pushed the door open.

The office was crowded. A metal desk, all dented and rust-flecked, sat in the center, covered with parts manuals, invoices, and magazines. Spare parts and other manuals were littered over the floor. The wall behind the desk was a big cork board covered with photos and newspaper clippings affixed with thumb tacks and tape. Some of the photos hung askew, or overlapped other photos.

The big guy stopped talking when I walked in, and gave me an appraising look. He turned back to the little guy. "Okay, Billy," he said. "We'll finish this little talk later." He turned back to me, smiling. "What can I do you for, mister?"

I showed him my ID. "I'm working on a case, and a former employee of yours is involved. I'd like to ask you a few questions if you don't mind."

He looked a little disappointed. Guess he thought I was looking for an expensive repair job.

"Sure, pal," he said. "Which former employee you talking about?"

"Jason Lane. I understand he was your bookkeeper for a while."

His lips turned down in distaste. "That little sumbitch. Yeah, he kept the books. Little fuck just quit on me – didn't even give notice."

"I guess that must have been inconvenient – having to find a new bookkeeper like that. You have any idea why he quit?"

He perched on the edge of the desk, not even bothering to offer me a seat. I looked around, and realized that, except for the chair behind his desk, there was no other place to sit.

"Naw, I don't know why he quit, really. I didn't mind about the bookkeeping. I got a cousin who can keep books, and he needed a job. No, what really frosted my ass was Jason was one of my best drivers.

I gave him a confused look.

"Oh, yeah," he said. "See, the repair business is just part of what I do, and not the main part. I got me a stable of dirt track drivers who can drive the hell out of stock cars. We enter races all up and down the eastern seaboard, and as far over as Tennessee, Alabama, and Kentucky. Jason was a natural. Ain't no car that boy can't drive."

"I ran a background check on him," I said. "There was no record of him driving race cars."

Now, it was his turn to look confused. "That don't make no sense. He was one of my winningest drivers." He snapped his fingers. "Oh, wait a minute, I'll bet I know why you didn't find nothing. He raced under the name Johnny Lightning. And, boy, he was as fast as lightning. Won three out of every four races he drove in, and came in second or third in the rest."

Click. Click. Click. More pieces falling into place. A driver coming from a side road in the dark, trying to run Greg Cheney off the road - could be, I thought. I'd need to ask Cheney if Lane knew he'd be coming back on that road at that time.

"You haven't seen him since he quit?"

"Nah," he said. "He came in here one morning with his Jeep all banged up. Said he'd hit a deer. Looked like it too. The front bumper and grille, and the hood were all banged up, and the windscreen was busted. They all had to be replaced. One of the other mechanics helped him put the new parts on, but he didn't even stay around long enough to paint 'em. Just drove off, and never came back."

Click. More pieces.

"Was his jeep all yellow?" I asked.

"Sure," he said, pointing to a crooked photo directly behind his desk. "You can see it in this picture."

The photo was of a smiling Jason Lane, standing in front of a '68 Mustang GT. He was wearing a racing coverall and holding a gold trophy in one hand, with a beautiful, underdressed blonde hanging on the other arm. What caught my eye, though, was the spot of yellow in the far background – a lemon yellow Jeep; yellow hood, yellow grille, and yellow bumpers. *Click!* Buster's words came back, "They found bright yellow paint on her body and clothing on the right side." More pieces falling into place.

"How well did you know Lane?" I asked.

"Pretty well, I'd say. He and my cousin Jimmy went to high school together."

"Did you know his family?"

"Not all that well," he said. "I saw his mom around now and then. She died when he was in his first year of high school, and his sister moved in."

"His sister, Albertina?"

"Yeah, I reckon that was her name, but she didn't like it. Preferred being called Tina. She didn't mix with folks much, though. Stayed to herself. She was some kind of artist or some shit like that."

"You mean fashion designer?"

"Yeah, that's it. She was always drawing dresses and shit. Some of it looked pretty good. Anyway, when Jason graduated and went out on his own, she just disappeared. No idea where she went. He went to the community college and got his degree in accounting and come to work for me. That's when I learned the kid could drive. So, he did both. Did the books two, three days a week, and drove in races, mostly on weekends. We were making good money from it. What's he doing now?"

I wasn't comfortable sharing too much information with him. "He's working for a guy in DC who hired me to do a background check on him," I said.

At this point, the whole thing had clicked into place in my mind. I knew who was behind the attempt to extort money from Rigg, and I knew why. One of the perpetrators was already behind bars. The other one had been right under my nose the whole time, and I'd ignored him.

I knew the why and the who, and all I had to do now was push that final piece into place. I thanked Daryl Jackson for his help and left. It was time for the final moves in a deadly game of chess that the chess master, Tina Wittmer, had been playing from her cell in Lorton.

Back in my car, I removed my cell phone from my jacket pocket and dialed Rigg's studio number. Tillie the receptionist answered, and I asked her to put Rigg on.

"Calvin Rigg," he said. "What can I do for you?"

"It's more like what I can do for you,

friend," I said. "I know who's trying to extort money from you, and I know why he's doing it."

"Who is it?" There was a note of excitement in his voice.

"I don't want to talk about it over the phone. I'll come to your studio. We can talk there."

I rang off and gunned the Volkswagen's engine.

The hunt was on.

21.

It took me forty minutes to drive from Gaithersburg to Georgetown. I pulled into the parking garage next to Rigg's studio. The first level was full, so I had to drive down to the second level, where I found a space near the back of the dimly lit garage.

While the first level, with its large entrance doors, got some light from outside to supplement the fitful light from the widely scattered fluorescent fixtures, the second level's dark gray concrete walls were mostly in shadow. A floor to ceiling concrete partition bisected the space, with two rows of parking on each side of it. There was no elevator up to the first level, just a stairwell in the front, a long walk from where I was forced to park.

As I walked along the row of cars all I

could hear was the sound of my footsteps on the concrete, water dripping somewhere in the distance, and the hum and rattle of pipes. The place had that musty smell of oil, exhaust fumes, and mildew common to enclosed, poorly ventilated spaces.

The roar of a car's engine, muffled at first, grew louder. I looked up. A halo of light was moving across the concrete wall, growing smaller and more intense. It quickly became two distinct circles, which elongated, as the vehicle made the turn from the ramp and around the center partition. In the dark, all I could see was the two bright lights coming toward where I stood in the center of the space between the rows of parked cars – growing larger. The roar of the engine was deafening now.

I stood still, gauging the speed of the oncoming vehicle. The engine roared louder. Whoever was driving had pressed the gas pedal. I didn't need a neon sign to know that I was the target of whoever was behind the wheel. Still, I waited. If you're thinking 'deer in headlights,' think again. I didn't want to move too early and give the shithead trying to splatter me against his grille a chance to adjust his aim. As the car got closer, even in the dim light, I could see the flash of yellow above the windshield. Lane must have been waiting for me.

When the oncoming Jeep was about ten feet away, and picking up speed, I jumped to the right, between a BMW and an Opel, twisting around to look around the rear of the Opel. Lane expertly spun the Jeep around the turn at the back, and roared toward the front on the other side of the concrete barrier.

I considered making a dash for the stairwell, but knew I was no match for his vehicle. Instead, I darted in and out between cars, making my way closer to the front. I was about four cars from my goal when the yellow jeep with the black hood pulled into the turn around the barrier and stopped. I could see that the left front bumper was crumpled – probably from his attempt on Cheney. He sat there with the engine idling. His car was between me and the stairwell. I couldn't even go back and use my own car to get out of the place – the Jeep blocked the only exit.

It would be necessary to change his perception of things.

"Lane," I yelled. "I know it's you, and I know what you've done and are trying to do. It's over, kid, so you might as well give up now."

He didn't respond. Of course, I didn't expect him to. That was just to make him think he knew where I was. As soon as I stopped talking, I slipped back to the concrete barrier and stepped up on the trunk of the Opel, jumped from there to the trunk of a large dark car I didn't recognize, and then into the back of a small pickup. I immediately eased over the edge of the pickup cargo wall and crouched down next to the rear of a gray Volvo. I waited quietly. All I could hear was the throaty hum of his engine.

Slowly I eased up until I was peering over the back of the Volvo. The Jeep hadn't moved.

"Time's running out kid," I said. "This is your last chance. Give up now, and I'll put in a good word for you with the cops. Make me work to bring you in, and you're on your own."

There was a creaking sound, followed by the bang of metal on metal. Then, I heard the scuffing sound of shoes on the concrete.

"You're not fooling me, Mr. Pennyback." Lane's voice came from just around the edge of the concrete partition, about two car widths and some inches from where I crouched. "Calvin told me all about you. About how you never carry a gun, and how you have this code of chivalry and shit. Well, *I* have a gun, and I don't believe in knighthood and junk like that. In fact, I won't have any problem at all putting a bullet in you."

He'd taken the bait. Now, I had to keep him talking.

"You might find it harder to do than you think," I said. "Killing someone's not as easy as they make it look in the movies."

I eased up and hefted myself slowly and quietly onto the Volvo's trunk. Easing across it, I slid down the side and move to the next car, a Chevy Malibu painted in blue with red and white racing stripes.

"Oh, it's not all that hard," he said.

"Sure, running someone over with a car, and in the dark – that's easy. And, I suppose it's easy to get an old lady drunk and turn a gas jet on. But, using a gun or knife on another person – that's a different matter. Killing a man when you're looking him in the eye is a whole new ball game."

As I talked, I crab walked toward the front of the car, making sure I was there for most of my little speech. For what I planned to do, it was important that he fix on where he thought I was.

He was silent for a long time. When he finally spoke, there was some hesitancy in his voice. "So . . . you know about them, do you?" Good, he was beginning to have doubts. "Tina said you were good. I guess she was right."

"Your sister, Tina," I said. "Tina Wittmer. She the one who put you up to this?"

Another long silence, then he coughed.

"How'd you find out about her?" he asked.

"It wasn't that difficult. I have a partner who can find out things about people that they sometimes don't even know about themselves. What I don't know, though, is why you're doing this."

I had an idea, but I wanted to get him talking so that I could get a fix on where he was standing.

"Hell, since you're gonna be dead in a few minutes, I guess it won't hurt to tell you."

It was working. I had him talking now. The difference between an amateur and a professional crook is that the pro does the job and moves on. An amateur just has to tell someone about it. And, the smarter they think they are, the more they feel compelled to tell someone so their smartness can be recognized.

"I'm not sure about that dead part, but I am curious."

He ignored my taunt. "You're right, you

know. It was Tina's idea. I've been visiting her since she was locked up – keeping her up on the news and such. Of course, she hears a lot in there. Amazing how much stuff gets into a prison. Anyway, she heard this dude Rigg was making it big, and she figured he was doing it off her designs that Honeywell stole. She wanted to make him pay for it."

"You were jacking him up for most of his money," I said. "Why threaten his employees? Why kill Stella Mason and Martha Frank?"

"Shit, man, she didn't want his damn money. She wanted the fucker to suffer. In order to make sure he suffered, I had to be on the inside. The only jobs I knew how to do was janitor or assistant – I flipped a coin, and the old lady came up. That one was easy, 'cause she always came to work so early. Caught her crossing the street in the dark one morning, 'wham!' nobody say me, and off I went. Banged up my ride a bit, but one of the boys at Daryl's place fixed it up for me real nice."

"Okay, I guess I can see that, but why kill Martha Frank?"

"I couldn't get at any of the models, and I needed to stick it to Rigg. He didn't see that Mason broad's death as connected. I knew Martha and Lisa sometimes hit the bars after work. I just waited until Lisa took off, and I followed Martha home. I took a bottle of vodka, 'cause I knew she was partial to it. Had to drink a lot of it with her, but she finally dozed off. The rest was easy."

"I'm guessing you went after Greg Cheney for the same reason – make Rigg feel guilty, make him suffer? But, how did you know where he'd be?"

"Yeah, you got that right. I knew where he'd be, because he told everybody before he left work that day. I knew coming back he'd have to use that road to get to his place, so I just waited for him. Son of a bitch saw me, though, and I just clipped him. It would have still worked though, if you hadn't come along and ruined things."

I had my fish on the line. It was time to reel him in.

"Okay, Jason," I said. "It's time to end this thing. I'm coming for you."

I kept my eyes on the end of the concrete wall, holding in place until I saw the unmistakable outline of a pistol – it looked like a Colt .45 automatic, the workhouse of the U.S. Army from the Philippine Insurrection to the Vietnam War. It packs a wallop. The slug can stop a man even if it doesn't hit a vital organ because it makes such a big hole going in and coming out. Of course, it has a powerful recoil and isn't easy to use unless you're a really experienced marksman. I was banking on Lane being an amateur.

I started easing toward the back of the car. The gun moved farther past the wall, held down at a slight angle. Another indication that he was an amateur – holding it out from his body like that. If I'd been any closer I could have snatched it from him.

Hitting a target with a pistol isn't as easy as they make it look on TV and in the movies. It's hard to do even under ideal conditions, and especially if the target is moving or fighting back. Hitting a moving target with a pistol like the .45 automatic is extremely hard. You have to contend with the recoil – damn thing kicks like a pissed off mule – which can sprain your wrist if you're not holding it correctly. Added to that, we were in a poorly lit, enclosed space. A .45 is a veritable hand cannon. The boom is loud, and in an enclosed space would be magnified. Finally, in the dim light, the muzzle flash that close to your face would be like having someone set off a flashbulb right in front of your eyes. I had a hunch that Jason Lane hadn't given much thought to any of this.

And, I was right.

As he came around the corner, he was

focusing on the front of the Malibu just as I'd planned. I stood slowly. Cloaked in shadows as I was, he hadn't seen me. I boosted myself onto the trunk of the Malibu, causing it to dip slightly.

He must have caught that movement out of the corner of his eye. He started swinging the .45 around toward me, bringing it up into firing position. I began moving forward as he did that – setting myself to jump forward onto the trunk of the last car. I launched myself. I felt a little bad, because that last car was a black Mercedes-Benz S-550, and I knew that my shoes would scuff the trunk when I landed. I hit the trunk with a thud, and a millisecond later, Lane pulled the trigger – a millisecond too soon. There was a flash, and a boom that echoed in my ears, and I felt the heat of 15 grams of lead zipping past at over 900 feet per second – almost close enough to singe my clothing. But, when you're shooting at someone, almost isn't good enough.

Lane was still semi-dazed as I made my final leap from the trunk of the Benz, landing in front of him. His eyes went wide as I grabbed the wrist of his gun hand with my left hand, pressing my thumb into a spot just below his thumb, cutting off circulation, and – I'm sure – hurting like hell. Before his brain could register the pain in his wrist, though, I brought my right fist back to a point opposite my right ear and drove it forward into the bridge of his nose. I *know* that hurt, because he squealed like a little girl, letting go of the .45 and grabbing his nose with both hands. Blood spurted between his fingers. I pocketed the pistol. Taking my time, I grabbed both his ears and pulled his head forward until he was bent ninety degrees at the waist. I then brought my right knee up, smashing it against his face – completing the ruination of his already mangled nose, and cracking his lips. I let go of his ears, and his head snapped back, pulling his body with it. He smashed against his Jeep, and slid down to a sitting position, his head dipped forward, blood from his nose and mouth dripping down the front of his tan jacket. He didn't notice any of this, though. He was out cold.

I pulled my cell phone from my pocket. The signal was weak, but I was able to dial 911.

22.

It didn't take the cops long to arrive. Buster came along with the patrol car. He'd been in the precinct when my call came in. When they first uniformed cop saw Lane's face, he turned and puked. A rookie. He'd see much worse if he stayed on the force long enough.

They hustled Lane into an ambulance, handcuffed to the stretcher, and took him off to the prison ward of DC General Hospital. A detective took my statement, paying special attention to the background information that explained why I was in the garage with Lane trying to kill me in the first place. They impounded his Jeep, and the next day Buster informed me that a sample of the yellow paint was taken and it matched exactly the paint on Stella Mason's body. They also matched the black paint on the crumpled fender against the black scratches on Greg Cheney's car – another match.

Lane was lucky that Mason's murder, the only one they had evidence to tie him to, had taken place in the District, which doesn't have the death penalty. He denied having admitted to me that he'd killed Frank, so technically that one remains unsolved. He'll get twenty to life, though, so he'll be paying for it, so I'm satisfied. Wittmer, the brains behind it all, won't be on the streets anytime soon either. When Lane confessed that he'd colluded with her against Rigg, the court added time to her sentence.

I can only wonder. If Lane had been successful in his attack on Rigg – would I have been next? I did, after all, play a significant role in putting Tina Wittmer behind bars, and she seemed to have an unhealthy appetite for revenge. I suppose I'll never know. I can't ask her. She had my name removed from her authorized visitor's list. Her list is down two names now. Jason Lane will soon be a convicted felon, housed in the same institution, but unable to have any contact with his half-sister. What a fitting punishment for both of them. And, when Lorton eventually closes, and the inmates are transferred, there's no guarantee they'll end up in the same place, putting even more distance between them.

Wittmer used her brother to try and destroy someone else. She ended up destroying her one remaining link to the outside world. Karma is a bitch.

Charles Ray

23.

Saturday, February 17, 2001 – by evening, the cold had set in, but the humidity was low for Washington, so it wasn't too uncomfortable. Nonetheless, Sandra and I bundled up. We were spending the evening out.

The parking garage next to the studio was jammed, not that I minded after my experience with Jason Lane, so we drove around until we found an empty space three blocks from the theater where Calvin Rigg was staging his fashion show. Sandra tucked her arm in mine and held her head against my shoulder as we walked back.

The foyer of the place was decorated with red, white, and blue balloons and photos from Rigg's previous shows. A large table, laden with hors d'ouevres and champagne, sat in the middle. A large group of people, the men in tuxes and the women in fancy gowns, crowded around it stuffing their faces with pate and cheese crackers, and slurping champagne. Sandra and I had left home early and stopped by the little Chinese restaurant on Travilah Road, so we passed on the snacks.

Rigg, dressed in mauve pants and a lilac shirt, over which he wore a beige sweater, was standing by one of the doors to the auditorium when we came in. When he saw us, he rushed over, kissing Sandra's cheek and grabbing my arm. His face was flush.

"Al, Sandra," he said. "So glad you guys could make it. Thanks to you, Al, we're gonna have a boffo show tonight."

I laughed. "Boffo? I thought that was the way they described Broadway shows?"

"Well, if things go well tonight, the next time you see my designs they'll be close to Broadway. There are at least four fashion houses here tonight."

"I'm so happy for you, Cal," Sandra said. "I hope you do well – heck, I *know* you'll do well. Your designs are fantastic."

Rigg looked at me, a momentary frown crossing his face. "Yeah," he said. "My designs are great, but there's more to it than that."

"What do you mean?" she asked.

"I – I didn't know it until Jason got caught. I mean, I guess I should have known, but I didn't think about it. Some of the designs that I've been using came from Franklin's estate, and they were actually done by Tina. If . . . if I'd known, I would've given her credit, and maybe all this wouldn't have happened. Stella and Marsha might still be alive."

A tear slid slowly down his cheek.

"Don't beat yourself up," I said. "There was no way you could have known Honeywell had been stashing Tina's designs."

"But, I *should* have known. I loved Franklin, but let's face it - the man had no morals when it came to this business. He would have cheated his mother to get ahead."

"Well, there's not much you can do about it now."

He got a funny look on his face. "Maybe, maybe not. Look, let me get you two seated. You're on the front row, at the end of the runway just like last time. Hope you don't mind."

Sandra blushed and smiled. I didn't mind. It put me where I could sneak out without stepping over people if it got boring.

A few people were already seated. A few more stepped over our feet to get seated. After about five minutes every seat was filled. A few minutes later, the house lights went down. A circle of pink light appeared on the stage.

Rigg, dressed now in a white tuxedo, walked out and stood in the circle of light. There was a scattering of applause. He held up his hands for quiet. When the hall was quiet, he looked down at me, a slight smile on his face.

"Ladies and gentlemen," he said in a soft voice. "I want to thank you all for coming tonight. We *all* want to thank you." He paused, taking a deep breath. His eyes were shining. "Tonight's show is dedicated to former members of my staff who are no longer with us, Stella Mason and Martha Frank. Except for a couple of you, those names don't mean anything, but trust me, without them, I wouldn't be here." There was polite applause. "We also wouldn't be here tonight if not for Al Pennyback, the best damn private detective in Washington, DC." A spotlight fell on me. The applause was a bit louder, even though they had no idea who I was. Sandra hugged my arm tightly. Rigg held up his hands again. "Finally – while most of the designs you see tonight are mine

– some of them were inspired by a former colleague who can't be with us to enjoy this show, Ms. Tina Wittmer, one of the best fashion designer I know – aside from yours truly, that is." The crowd responded with laughter and applause. "Thank you again, and please enjoy the show."

The spotlight went out. When it was replaced by a general orange glow illuminating the runway, Rigg was gone. Soft music wafted from hidden speakers. A model strutted from behind the curtains on the right of the stage, and at the same time, one came from the left. Bibi Gunn, dressed in a white sheer number that displayed her body to best advantage came from the left, and Michelle Mignon, wearing a black mini-dress that matched the color of her hair, came from the right. They met in the center, grasped hands, and strolled down the runway together.

The crowd went wild.

"Why are they so excited," I whispered to Sandra.

"I don't think anyone's ever opened a show with *two* models before," she said. "It's . . . it's revolutionary. I can see why Calvin's so popular."

I shrugged and smiled. Rigg was a class act. He'd skillfully ducked the problem of which model would open the show, and gained a reputation for innovation in the process. I had to give him credit for that move. But, I really had to give him credit for giving credit to Tina's contribution to his designs. That took a big man. I could only hope word would get to her in her cell. If she'd told him about her designs in the first place, there would have been no need for Mason and Frank to die. Sometimes, taking the simple approach is the best way to solve a problem.

24.

Three days later, I received a summons to appear in Fairfax County Court.

I wasn't been accused of anything. Consolidated Insurance had decided to make an example of Wilmont Haverford. The company filed suit against him for filing a false claim, and I'd been called as a witness for the plaintiff.

Consolidated's attorney had decided to call me last, as he said, the cherry atop the dessert. I arrived at the courthouse at 9:00 a.m., and was directed to a bench just outside the courtroom, where I waited alone until 11:00, when the bailiff stuck his head out the door.

"You Albert Pennyback?" he asked. I nodded. "You're on."

I rose and followed him into the

courtroom. The place was pretty full. People come to see the rich guy get his comeuppance, I suppose. I walked down the center aisle, and to the witness stand to the right of the judge's bench. The judge, a portly woman with iron gray hair, smiled down at me. The bailiff administered the oath – 'the truth, the whole truth, and nothing but the truth' – to which I agreed.

The Consolidated attorney, a gaunt man with craggy features that made him look like Abe Lincoln without a beard, stepped up to face me.

"Would you please identify yourself, what you do, and your connection with this case," he said.

"Al, er, Albert Pennyback. I'm a private investigator, licensed in DC. Maryland, and Virginia. I was hired to look into an insurance claim filed by Mr. Wilmont Haverford."

"When you were hired, what were you told about the case?"

"I was just told to look into it to determine if it was valid."

"Were you told why?"

"Well, no – just that it was a rather large claim and the company wanted to make sure it was a good claim," I said.

"And, Mr. Pennyback, what did you find?" He turned and looked at the twelve members of the jury, who looked bored by the whole thing.

"Well, at first, it seemed like a valid claim," I said. "But, there were a few inconsistencies that bothered me."

"Can you tell us the nature of these *inconsistencies*?"

I described my thoughts about the convenient timing of the power outage with the failure of Haverford's home alarm system backup power, and the fact that he owned a company that did electrical contracting. Then I pointed out how I'd witnessed the argument between him and his wife over the missing paintings. "None of these, in and of themselves, point to a phony claim, but there were just too many coincidences. I reported that view to the insurance company."

The jury was leaning forward now. I had their interest, and the company lawyer loved it. Haverford and his lawyer, a short, bald man with an overbite, were looking glum.

"What else did you do?"

"Nothing," I said. "I was asked to look into it, and I did. My job was done when I reported it."

"Thank you, Mr. Pennyback," he said. He

turned to Haverford's lawyer. "Your witness, counselor."

The lawyer stood, adjusting his jacket. He walked slowly toward the witness stand, staring at me. He had to look up at me.

"Tell me, Albert, you mind if I call you Albert –"

"My friends call me Al," I said. "And, we just met."

"Mr. Carson, we'll have decorum in my court," the judge said. "You will address the witness appropriately."

His cheeks reddened. "Yes, your honor," he said. "Well, *Mr.* Pennyback, I have only one question – were you paid for your services in this case?"

"Yes," I said.

"Could you be a bit more specific? Just how much were you paid?"

"I'm paid a retainer by Holcombe, Stein and Chang, the law firm that represents Consolidated Insurance. In addition, after I'd submitted my report, and the company denied the claim, I was told that I'd be paid ten percent of the claim amount."

"And, just how much was that ten percent?"

"Two hundred thousand dollars."

A couple of the jurors gasped audibly.

"Really? Quite an incentive to find that the claim was bogus, wouldn't you say?"

The little pantywaist was accusing me of shading an investigation for money – of cheating. I felt like grabbing him by the throat and shaking him until his eyes popped out. But, I realized that he was just doing his job of representing his client aggressively, even though his client was a cheating dirt bag. I took a slow breath before answering.

"I was not told of the bonus until after I'd completed my investigation," I said simply.

He blinked. I think he thought his question would fluster me and cause me to respond emotionally. Score one for Al Pennyback. I don't do emotional. But, he wasn't done yet.

"Come on, Mr. Pennyback," he said. "Surely you knew that you'd get a percentage of whatever you saved the company."

"I've never worked for an insurance company before. As far as I knew, I was working for my normal retainer."

He blinked again. I almost felt sorry for the poor schmuck. He didn't know who he was dealing with. I've faced down terrorists with AK-47s, who wanted nothing more than to put a few new holes in my body. And, I did it all without blinking. He didn't stand a chance.

"Your honor," the insurance company lawyer said. "My learned opponent has asked the same question, albeit in a slightly different way, twice and gotten the same answer. He is perilously close to badgering the witness."

"What are you objecting to, Mr. Turnbull?" the judge asked in a dry tone.

"Oh, no objection – yet – your honor," he said. "But, I should think Mr. Callum has asked all of his questions by now."

The judge sniffed, but turned to Callum, who was standing in front of me looking combative. "Mr. Turnbull's intervention was out of order, Mr. Callum, but he does make a point. Do you have any more *relevant* questions, and by that, I don't mean any more questions about whether or not the witness knew about the insurance company bonus. I think he has adequately answered that."

Callum's cheeks blossomed – the color of roses. "Uh, yes, your honor," he said. "I have no further questions."

"You're excused, Mr. Pennyback," the

judge said.

My civic duty done, I went back to my office. There wasn't much to do. It's often like that after a case. We sit around waiting for the next one, Heather doing whatever it is she does with her computer, and me staring out the window or masochistically playing computer chess.

The phone rang around 3:00 in the afternoon.

"Boss, it's someone named Turnbull," Heather said. "Said he had some news for you. Shall I put him through?"

I told her he was the insurance company lawyer and asked that he be put through.

"Mr. Pennyback," he said. "I just thought you'd like to know – the jury found in our favor. Not only will Haverford have the claim denied, but he'll pay damages and court costs. I heard the state is considering prosecuting him for filing a false police report. I have to say, it was your calm, cool testimony that put us over the top. Thanks."

"Just doing my job," I said.

"And a good job it was. Most people would have been rattled by Callum's attacks. You just seemed to get calmer the more he probed. He's still reeling from it. Anyway, thanks for your help."

He rang off. I sat back in my chair, looking up at the ceiling. It was simple really. Keep your eye on your objective, and don't let yourself be sidetracked or flustered.

Simple is always best.

Drop Dead, Gorgeous

Charles Ray

Books by this author:

Al Pennyback mysteries

Color Me Dead
Memorial to the Dead
Deadline
Dead, White, and Blue
A Good Day to Die
The Day the Music Died
Die, Sinner
Deadly Intentions
Death by Design
Till Death Do Us Part
Deadly Dose
Dead Man's Cove
Dead Men Don't Answer
Deadly Paradise
Kiss of Death
Death in White Satin
Death and Taxis
Drop Dead, Gorgeous

The Buffalo Soldier series:

Buffalo Soldier: Trial by Fire
Buffalo Soldier: Homecoming
Buffalo Soldier: Incident at Cactus Junction
Buffalo Soldier: Peacekeepers
Buffalo Soldier: Renegade
Buffalo Soldier: Escort Duty
Buffalo Soldier: Yosemite
Buffalo Soldier: Battle at Dead Man's Gulch

Other fiction

Angel on His Shoulder
She's No Angel
Child of the Flame
Pip's Revenge
Wallace in Underland
Further Adventures of Wallace in Underland
Dead Letter and Other Tales
The White Dragons
The Dragon's Lair
The Last Gunfighters
The Culling
Frontier Justice: Bass Reeves, Deputy U.S. Marshal

Nonfiction

Things I Learned from My Grandmother About Leadership and Life
Taking Charge: Effective Leadership for the Twenty-first Century
Grab the Brass ring
African Places: A Photographic Journey Through Zimbabwe and southern Africa
There's Always a Plan B
A Portrait of Africa

About the Author

Charles Ray has been writing fiction since his teens. He won a Sunday school magazine writing contest when he was thirteen, and having his byline on a short story published in a national publication forever hooked him on writing. During his time in the army (1962-1982) he often moonlighted as a newspaper or magazine journalist, and was the editorial cartoonist for the Spring Lake (NC) News, a weekly newspaper, during the 1970s. In addition to his writing, he was an artist/cartoonist and photographer for a number of publications, including Ebony, Eagle and Swan, and Essence, and had a monthly cartoon feature and did several covers for Buffalo, a now-defunct magazine that was dedicated to showcasing the contributions of African-Americans to the country's military history.

After retiring from the army, he joined the U.S. Foreign Service, and served as a diplomat in posts in Asia and Africa until his retirement in 2012. He has worked and traveled throughout the world (Antarctica is the only continent he hasn't visited), and now, as a full time writer, continues to globetrot looking for interesting things to write about, draw, or take pictures of.

A native of Texas, he now calls Maryland home. For more on his writing and other projects, check one of the following Web sites:

http://redroom.com/member/charles-a-ray
http://charlesaray.blogspot.com
http://charlieray45.wordpress.com
http://www.twitter.com/charlieray45
http://www.facebook.com/charlieray45
http://www.flickr.com/photos/charlesray45/
http://www.viewbug.com/member/charlesray

www.ingramcontent.com/pod-product-compliance
Lightning Source LLC
Chambersburg PA
CBHW060139130626
46556CB00006B/2413